# CLUTTER BUSTERS
## "It takes more time to be messy than it does to be neat."

**Household Fact:** Chocolate is very difficult to get out of computer keyboards.

**Household Fact:** Licking the keyboard is not an option.

**Suggestion:** Eat M&M's. They melt in your mouth, not in your keyboard.

**Household Hint:** Put all appointments on calendar as soon as you schedule them.

**Household Fact:** Calendar has gone AWOL.

**Suggestion:** Use paper towels to hold information instead.

**Household Hint:** Leftover chocolate chips should be stored in a sealed container for maximum freshness.

**Household Fact:** Leftover chocolate chips?

**Books by Judy Baer**

Love Inspired

*Be My Neat-Heart* #347

Steeple Hill Women's Fiction

*The Whitney Chronicles*
*Million Dollar Dilemma*

## JUDY BAER

"Angel" Award winning author and two-time RITA®
Award finalist Judy Baer has written more than
seventy books in the past twenty years, including
the bestselling Cedar River Daydreams series, with
over 1.25 million copies in print. Her next Steeple
Hill single title will be *Norah's Ark*, to be published
in September 2006. A native of North Dakota and
graduate of Concordia College in Minnesota, she
currently lives near Minneapolis. In addition to writing,
Judy works as a personal life coach and writing coach.
Judy speaks in schools, churches, libraries, women's
groups and at writers' workshops across the country.
She enjoys time with her husband, two daughters, three
stepchildren and the growing number of spouses, pets
and babies they bring home. Judy, who once raised
buffalo, now raises horses. Readers are invited to visit
her Web site at www.judykbaer.com.

# Be my
## neat-heart

# JUDY BAER

Steeple
Hill®

Published by Steeple Hill Books™

STEEPLE HILL BOOKS

Steeple
Hill®

ISBN 0-373-87367-0

BE MY NEAT-HEART

Copyright © 2006 by Judy Duenow

www.SteepleHill.com

**Printed in U.S.A.**

Do not store up for yourselves treasures on earth, where moth and rust consume and where thieves break in and steal. But store up for yourselves treasures in heaven, where neither moth nor rust consumes and where thieves do not break in and steal. For where your treasure is, there your heart will be also.

—*Matthew* 6:19–21

For Dr. Priscilla Herbison, in recognition of her efforts to find the very best in her students.

# Chapter One

*A girl could get killed on a job like this.*

I dived out of the way as an avalanche of Tupperware fell out of Mrs. Fulbright's cupboard directly toward my head. In my escape I tripped on a cardboard box full of parts-missing appliances and barely caught myself on the cluttered kitchen counter. The woman owns more foam meat trays than a chain of butcher shops and every margarine tub that ever crossed her threshold. Not only that, I'm considering nominating her for the Cool Whip Container Hall of Fame.

"You aren't planning to throw *those* out, are you?" Mrs. Fulbright peered doubtfully into a stack of the plastic bowls. In the top bowl the carcass of a house fly was resting in peace. It was clear she hadn't had these out of the cupboard since Granny of *The Beverly Hillbillies* and the transplanted socialite on *Green Acres* were homemaking role models. "I've been thinking of taking up watercolor painting. I'll need them to wash out my brushes."

*Maybe. If you're recreating the ceiling of the Sistine Chapel on the roof of the Metrodome.*

"Remember the vision you created for yourself, Mrs. Fulbright?" I asked gently. "The dream you've always had?"

She looked at me glassy-eyed, her attention still fixed on the hundreds of ways old food containers could be made into soap dishes, shower slippers and patio furniture. Simple as it might seem to others, wrenching these years of accumulation away from her was a little like ripping out her heart. Even though she'd hired me to do it, it had to be done with compassion. My job as a professional organizer is part coach, champion, cheerleader, friend, objective thinker and part cleaning lady. Interesting, isn't it, how God designs us for a purpose? For me, an incorrigible neatnik, this is the perfect occupation.

*I love it when He does this stuff.*

"'Vision'? Oh, yes. Never again being hit on the head with an aluminum pie plate," she parroted without conviction. "No more stacking glasses five deep and being unable to pull them apart. Room for the set of dishes my daughter gave me for Christmas. No more stitches in my head when serving platters fall on me." She looked longingly at the yellowed plastic containers with which she'd bonded. "But it seems like such a waste to throw them away."

"Don't worry." I opened another cupboard to reveal a stash of empty squeezable bears, the kind honey comes in. "You'll still have these."

When I pulled away from the Fulbrights', my car was full of black lumpy garbage bags. In serious cases like that of Mrs. Fulbright, I always take the garbage bags away with me so as to prevent my client from having a panic attack in the night and rescuing the detritus.

*Samantha Is My Name, Busting Clutter Is My Game....*
I scratched out that line in my notebook and tried again.

*In Two Hours or Less I'll Un-muddle Your Mess....*
False advertising.
*Tired of being left out of the neatness game? Call Samantha Smith, professional Clutter Coach.*

Too kitschy?
*Got Chaos? Call Clutter Busters!*

"What are you doing, Sam?" My receptionist/secretary/Jill-of-all-trades/clutter-buster-in-training Theresa Wilcox stooped to peer over my shoulder as I wrote.

"I'm trying to create a catchy tagline for a radio advertisement. I'm buying time during the morning commute starting next Monday, targeting harassed commuters who are running late because they couldn't find their kids' homework, their shoes or their briefcases."

"So you're after ninety percent of the country's working population?" Theresa snapped her ever-present chewing gum. "This morning I couldn't even find my *kid.* How was I supposed to know that Hannah had packed her own lunch and was waiting for me in the car?"

"Maybe I hired the wrong member of your family," I sighed. Theresa is a gem, but she's not naturally gifted with the neatness gene that runs in my family. By the time I was five years old, I could sort laundry—polyester and cotton, whites, darks, reds, denims, delicates and towels—and tell the difference between the mushroom soup and the tomato and put them in their appropriate places in the pantry. I also had my Barbie doll's clothing sorted by season, event—dressy, casual, dates with Ken—and color. I still miss poor old Ken. I can't believe she broke up with him after all these years.

Or maybe I'm just jealous that a plastic doll with bubble hair has a better social life than I do. I admire Barbie's panache and boldness—dumping Ken and all—but I'm the kind of woman who sticks to what she knows. I've always played it safe and a little boring in the romance department. That's probably a commentary on my whole life. Being a professional organizer and clutter coach is a manifestation of my liking to have my world in order. Better safe than sorry is my motto. How pathetic is that?

"Want to hear what's on your agenda this week?" Theresa handed me a printout. "Mrs. Fulbright called. She was wondering if you'd already disposed of those garbage bags. Her neighbor told her about a way to make bird feeders out of the bleach bottles and she's having thrower's remorse."

Mrs. Fulbright thinks she wants to put her life in order but she's still having a love affair with her junk.

"What's this?" I pointed to today's three o'clock time slot. *Carver Advertising—consultation requested.* I was hoping to go home early and take a quick nap before dinner. I'd spent the entire night before dreaming about organizing the bathroom of a client who owns more inventory than Walgreens. Every time I turned my back on her makeup drawers, eyeliners would leap in with the lipsticks and cotton balls, and makeup sponges would proliferate like dust bunnies under a bed.

I'm an organizational consultant and clutter coach. What am I supposed to dream about, Brad Pitt?

"I'm not sure. A secretary called this morning and asked that you were to be there *promptly* at three—or else."

"Did she really say 'or else'?" I put a stray paper clip back in its appropriate container and flipped to a fresh page in my notebook. Theresa says my desk is a metaphor for my life—perfectly ordered, immaculately clean and totally predictable. I've thought of challenging her on that but, unfortunately, most of it is true. I'd like to think I'm at least a tiny bit unpredictable.

"She might as well have. You'd have thought she was setting up an audience with the Queen." Theresa's expression brightened. "Maybe you'll be hired to organize an entire company."

Theresa has great pipe dreams. Unfortunately, people usually don't realize how much they need me until they lose something really important, like the deed to their house or their diamond earrings. Then, unless they agree to clutter coaching and a class or two, as soon I come in to reorder their lives, they find the misplaced items and revert to their messy ways. You've definitely got to change a messie from the inside out.

A lightbulb went on in my brain.

*Let Samantha Smith, organizational consultant and clutter coach, organize your world from the inside out!*

# Chapter Two

My cell phone rang for the umpteenth time. "Your clutter is my business. May I help you?"

"How's my sweet little cluttermeister?" An amused voice tickled my eardrum. "Want some lunch?"

That teasing voice gets me every time. Picturing Benjamin Rand's soft curly brown hair, five o'clock shadow and crooked smile, I could practically hear him reeling me in. Still, I tried to resist. "Can't. I don't have time. I have an appointment this afternoon. A *consultation*. With a *corporation*."

Ben was typically unimpressed. "Stuffed shirts, brain-washed heads, robotic activities, corporate clutter. Cool. *Not*."

"Ben…"

"Besides, I've already got it cooked—almost. It will be ready when you get there. It's on The Timer."

"You know what happened last time you used The Timer…."

"Mere technical difficulty. I've addressed the fire safety issue. There will be no more fire trucks on the lawn or hoses in the living room, I promise."

One could only have this conversation with Ben and have it make sense.

"Be here in twenty minutes and a gourmet feast awaits you."

And without waiting for my reply, he hung up.

Knowing he'd already decided I was coming and would refuse to pick up the telephone again, I succumbed to the lure of another meal made without the use of human hands.

Ben's place, a cozy bungalow-style house in south Minneapolis, is a solid, fifty-year-old stucco. It's a three-bedroom, single-bath home as typically traditional on the outside as it is atypical on the inside. I've known Ben for five years—ever since he bought the charmingly squat little house from my great aunt Gertie. Gertie, who feared being a "burden to family" in her old age, sold the house, bought a loft downtown and took off on a cruise of indefinite length. So far Gertie hasn't been a burden to anyone but Arthur Mason, the sweet seventysomething man she met in the cruise exercise class and promptly married.

Aunt Gertie has embraced this, her first marriage, like a bride fifty years younger. Poor Arthur has been the victim of Gertie's healthy cooking (miso soup, flounder and roasted cauliflower are her specialties), her constant redecorating of their loft (she's in an ultracontemporary phase right now and there is not a soft or rounded edge in the place) and healthy living (Arthur is currently enrolled in a kick-boxing class). When I'm her age, I want to be just like her.

The house must have a force field around it that attracts eccentrics. Otherwise, how could one home get two of them in a row—first Aunt Gertie and now Ben, who, among his other distinctions is a physicist, research scientist, inventor and inveterate chess player?

He's also a great friend. My mother wishes he were my boyfriend, but it's not going to happen. Ben's very much an "in the moment" type guy. He has to be. He'd probably blow himself up if he weren't paying attention at all times.

It comforts my mother to think that her nearly thirty-year-old daughter has a man in her life, so I don't burst her bubble and tell her that there is not even a remote possibility it could be Ben. Fortunately, or unfortunately, Mom and Dad live in Florida now, where Dad is president of a small Christian college, so she's not available for constant romantic input.

I love Ben, but I don't *love* Ben. He's a "space saver," like one of those promise rings young men give their girlfriends to wear on the ring finger of their left hands to save the space for something bigger and more permanent, like an engagement ring. Ben, who is a gem himself, is holding that space in my life right now. Frankly, I'm not sure if there is a diamond of a man out there for me. I worry about that sometimes—but not enough to do anything about it.

I jogged up the walk and entered the house without knocking. Ben bounded toward me and grabbed my hand. "Come see The Timer, it is operational."

Ben's working on an extension of the self-timing oven, the kind you can program to start cooking supper while you're still at work. Ben's not satisfied with a mere oven, however. He's invented a device that, in theory at least, will control all one's kitchen gadgets—or any set of electrical appliances—at once. Ben grew up with a mother who had difficulty getting the meat, potatoes and vegetables to the table hot at the same time. I think it damaged his psyche in some small way.

As we walked into the kitchen, the alarm rang on the oven, a radio began to play, coffee began to brew, water started to run in the sink and two pieces of toast sprang from the toaster and landed on the counter.

"Too much force," Ben muttered. "I'll adjust that after lunch. There's soup in the Crock-Pot, a cake in the oven and your toast is—" he gestured toward the counter "—there."

Ben loves to fool around with electricity and he plays with it much too often. He's finally promised me that he will never use The Timer on the electric mixer, heating pads, the electric chain saw or the egg poacher ever again. He's tried and it wasn't pretty.

I dished up the soup while he slathered canned frosting on the too-hot cake and it melted into the top, making a strange, lumpy glaze.

"Why do you keep fooling with this thing?" I asked as I dipped my finger into the odd-looking frosting. "If someone wants a fully electronic house, they can already buy it that way. Aren't you reinventing the wheel?"

"It's fun," he said cheerfully. "Besides, it's not the destination, it's the journey."

I suppose there can't be much fun in writing a book on quantum-something-or-other, which he's doing right now. He's got to enjoy life somehow.

Ben's almost too bright for his own good. He likes me because I'm levelheaded, down-to-earth and pragmatic, qualities that do not run freely in his family's DNA. Intelligence, however, is rampant. Ph.D. could be a pet family nickname, since everyone in his clan had one behind his or her name. Most of the Rands live life in the cloistered halls of higher education. None of them, however, can work an iPod, and they all get a deer-in-the-headlights look if I mention something as mundane as watching network television.

Not one of them understands that I enjoy making a living organizing other people's closets and coaching them to become their highest and best selves. Nor can the Rands comprehend that one can actually become certified and credentialed in such an endeavor. They'd all feel better if I said I were working on a project to reorder the thinking processes of homo sapiens between the ages of twenty and sixty with the intent of creating natural anxiety suppressants. Now *that's* something they could get their minds around.

"Are you going to church tonight?" I asked as I sipped my lukewarm soup. Ben and I often go together. I think of church as a sort of umbilical cord between me and God. The church—because of the preaching and teaching of His word and the fellowship I find there—is where I go for nutrients. It's one of my spiritual feeding stations, and I'm always hungry for God.

Ben teaches Sunday school, and I, among other things, occasionally volunteer in the nursery. Thanks to a few long stints in the crying room, I understand why my married friends say that spending a few hours with squalling babies is a great form of birth control. It certainly silences my biological time clock. After having my eardrums pierced by a colicky baby, I can't hear a tick or a tock for days.

He looked up sharply. "Is it Sunday already?" Ben also has difficulty with the calendar.

"No, silly. It's Wednesday. There's a concert."

"Wednesday? I have a meeting at the university. Thanks for reminding me."

He dished up a piece of cake the size of Rhode Island and put it in front of me. "How did yesterday go?"

"As well as can be expected, considering my client was born in the late 1930s and had parents who lived through the Depression."

Ben nodded sagely. "Couldn't get her to throw anything out, huh?"

"She grew up with nothing, and is determined either consciously or subconsciously not to let that happen again. People like Mrs. Fulbright fight scarcity piece by piece, container by container. She's saved everything. I have to be gentle."

Ben leaned forward and chucked me under the chin like I

was his favorite Irish setter. "You can't be anything but gentle, Sammi. You don't know how."

Maybe I don't know how to be anything but gentle, but by the time I got to Carver Advertising through downtown traffic, two full parking garages, ten miles of skyway, a maze of gate-keepers, a handful of low-level minions and a bossy executive secretary, I was willing to learn.

What made it even worse was the handsome but fuming, ill-tempered man I rode up with in the elevator. He repeatedly punched the already lit button to the 23$^{rd}$ floor and tapped his toe at what he obviously viewed as an extraordinarily slow closing door. The elevator stopped at several floors, and at each one he scowled ferociously at those who entered. Everyone was able to escape his apparent temper by the 21$^{st}$ floor except me, so he glowered at me as if the entire leisurely elevator ride were my fault.

Too bad he was such a grouch. He would have been downright gorgeous without the scowl. He had dark hair, a nicely tanned complexion and eyes the color of a violet-blue sea. I didn't see his smile, of course, but unless he was a real Snagglepuss, he was first rate in the looks department.

He darted out of the elevator and down the hall even before I got a chance to look at the building directory listing the office number for Carver Advertising.

*Lord, here we are. As always, I ask that I be Your representative as I meet new clients. Let Your light shine in me. Amen.*

I've discovered that business is always better with God as a consultant. His services come free of charge, and He's never wrong. What better advisor could I have than that?

After a trip to the powder room to spruce up, I entered Suite 2307. A secretary looked me up and down skeptically, clearly wondering what purpose I could serve. People sometimes respond to me that way. It's probably because I'm blond. Really blond. So blond that others assume those blond jokes were actually written about me. I smiled reassuringly at the receptionist and took a seat.

When I was a child my hair was nearly white. I was so fair that my parents insist they were forced to spend my inheritance on sunscreen and umbrellas. I blame my Nordic roots, the ones that also gave me rosy cheeks and wintry blue eyes. Much as I hate to admit it, I do look a little…well…Barbie-like, all fluff, no substance. I've spent much of my life dispelling that notion.

The other gift from my ancestors is more useful. I'm tall, long-legged and athletic. I work out a little and look like I work out a lot. And I've been skiing since I was five, when my father took me to Buck Hill and got me hooked. Skiing is great for every muscle group I own.

I sat back in my chair and looked around. Nice digs. A good gig if you could get it. Original artwork on the walls, carpet with a variety of colors cut into it to make the swooping design *CA,* for Carver Advertising, on the floor.

There wasn't a tired, out-of-date magazine, a stray dust mote or a streak on the bank of windows overlooking the city. There was nothing on the secretary's polished mahogany desk but the mandatory telephone and computer equipment, a few sheets of paper and a fountain pen. I couldn't begin to imagine what it was these people wanted organized.

It had been a long day, I realized as I waited for my summons into the inner sanctum of Carver Advertising. I rarely have the opportunity to sit down in a clutter-free environment that's not of my own making. It's very relaxing for a person who loves orderliness. I closed my eyes, relishing the tidiness and serenity that cocooned me. Unfortunately it was so relaxing that I nearly dozed off.

When I heard a man clear his throat and speak my name, I jumped to my full five-foot-nine-inch height—five-eleven if I count the heels—and gave a startled, unfortunately loud squawk.

Not cool, I thought to myself as I gathered my scattered wits about me.

"Oh, ah…sorry…it was so calm and quiet in here…too many Cool Whip containers…never mind…." I thrust out my hand. "Samantha Smith, organizational consultant. Let me help you organize your world."

The man, his brown hair prematurely shot with gray, looked at me in bemusement. He was clean shaven in the way of men who use straight-edged razors rather than electric ones, and his well-scrubbed apple cheeks gleamed. He was round in a Has-The-Makings-of-a-Santa-Claus-Someday way, and his light green eyes twinkled.

"Miss Smith, my name is Ethan Carver. Thank you for coming on such short notice." He eyed me with what was either amusement or indigestion. "I can see that your time must be consumed by many things."

Totally embarrassed, I followed him into his office. If I were my dog, Imelda, my tail would have been between my legs. Imelda's tail is between her legs a lot, mostly because she lives up to her name.

Imelda, one of those "designer" dogs, a labradoodle, is a cross between a Labrador and a poodle. Imelda loves shoes. Adores them. She will eat as many as she can find. I didn't discover the depth and breadth of her shoe fetish until I'd had her nearly three months. I simply thought that I was forgetting my heels at the gym after work, and when I went back for them, they'd already walked off. The one place in my house that I do not clean weekly is under my bed. I have moveable storage compartments there, which I move only seasonally when I change my clothes from winter to summer and vice versa. Imagine my shock, then, when I pulled out those containers to discover a horrific shoe cemetery in the space behind my winter clothes.

It took me days to get over the fact I'd been sleeping over a graveyard—the sad, strange, lonely place my shoes had gone to die.

Imelda, the heartless fiend, however, was overjoyed to have easier access to the remains of her prey and walked around for the rest of day with an amputated three-and-a-half-inch heel from my one and only pair of Manolo Blahniks in her mouth.

Once a shoe lover, always a shoe lover, I guess.

# *Chapter Three*

Carver's office was pristine—to the naked eye, at least.

I sat down awkwardly in a contemporary, geometrically designed chair that had nothing to do with the shape of the human body unless, of course, you were the model for Picasso's *Sitting Woman With the Green Scarf.*

"Now you know my weakness, Mr. Carver. I work too many hours and sleep on the job. How about you?"

"My Achilles' heel may not be quite as visible as yours, Ms. Smith, but present and accounted for nonetheless."

"I must admit I'm not familiar with Carver Advertising," I began. Listening is half my job, discovering who people really are and what they're about.

"We handle several large sports-related advertising accounts. We're big into baseball right now." He studied me carefully. "Now tell me what *you* do."

"I empower people to unburden themselves of life's excess baggage and to live in freedom, simplicity and order." The elevator speech rolled off my tongue with ease, the result of a thousand repetitions.

His eyes widened and I added, "Frankly, sir, as my thirteen-year-old neighbor says rather crassly, I help people 'get their poop in a group.' I help them prioritize, organize and sanitize. I help them categorize, systematize and standardize...." Oh, oh, I was on a roll. "I show them how to purify, classify and stupefy...." I pulled myself together before I burst into "the knee bone is connected to the thigh bone...."

"Sorry, I get carried away putting like things together—even words."

Carver grinned, but a disparaging snort from somewhere over my right shoulder made me flinch. I spun around to see the handsome, bad-tempered man from the elevator leaning against a bookcase, a coffee mug in his hand and a withering expression on his features.

He stared at me as if I were Kafka's cockroach lounging on the miserably uncomfortable chair, a chair only my Aunt Gertie could love. I squirmed as any self-respecting bug might. "You!" I blurted before my brain was in gear. "From the elevator!"

"You two have met?" Carver seemed astonished by that.

"We rode up together in the elevator," I stammered.

"The one that stopped at every floor?" Now Carver really looked amused. Then he seemed to remember there were amenities to perform.

"Ms. Smith, I'd like you to meet my friend, Jared Hamilton. Jared just stopped by to—" he paused to choose his words carefully "—to vent about something concerning his work. I invited him to stay and see what you had to say. Do you mind?"

I minded a great deal, but I didn't think it was prudent to say as much. "Anyone you choose to have here is welcome, Mr. Carver." I turned to face the desk again but had the sense that Hamilton was hovering above me like a bad-tempered bat hanging from the rafters. Granted, a good-looking bat, with chiseled features and broad shoulders, but he alarmed me nonetheless. Too serious. Too cantankerous.

Carver smiled encouragingly, as if to tell me to ignore the storm cloud lurking in the corner. "I don't believe I've ever met anyone quite like you before, Ms. Smith," Carver said.

I didn't dare consider what he might mean by that, so I decided to take it as an admiring comment. A girl can use all the compliments she can get.

Unfortunately, I heard a muttered "No kidding?" from behind me.

"Pay no attention to him," Carver said, giving Jared Hamilton a dirty look. "He's had some bad financial news, and he's being rather loutish at the moment."

"Yes…well." *Excessively loutish, if you ask me.*

"Now that we've settled that, Mr. Carver, why am I here?" I forced bat-man out of my mind. "What can I do for you? This office doesn't appear to need a professional organizer."

Silently he stood up and moved toward the bank of mahogany doors that lined the wall behind his desk. Without comment, he opened them.

Why he wasn't buried in an avalanche of paper as the doors silently slid away, I'll never know. Shades of those sneaky Pharisees! With Ethan Carver, what you see is not exactly what you get. The cup—or in this case, the closet—had not been cleaned in a very long time.

"This will be our little secret, Ms. Smith. You do have a confidentiality clause in your contract, don't you?"

I made a little zippering motion across my lips. No one would believe it, anyway. The papers looked like they'd been sorted by a wind machine. If there was any sense whatsoever to the mess, I couldn't fathom it.

"I'm known in my business as a perfectionist. I have a photographic memory and can retain virtually all of the details of my business up here." He pointed to his head. "Therefore, I seldom worry about the papers on which information is written and tend to simply toss them in here to be filed some day, but it has…gotten out of hand.

"My secretary does not deal with anything in my personal office. I prefer to do that myself." He cleared his throat. "Now it's to a point where I don't feel comfortable asking her." He began to pace a bit, the only sign of how this disturbed him.

"Because the company has grown, I've taken on a partner who will be on site starting next week. I prefer that he not see—" he gestured toward the mounds of floor-to-ceiling papers, files and flotsam and jetsam "—these."

I nodded mutely, already mentally shopping for file cabinets and ring-binder notebooks. This was the perfect job for an über-organizer like me.

Then I realized what he had said. "Next week?" I managed. "So soon?"

"You can do it, can't you?"

"But my other clients, well, I guess…sure."

"Good. Do you want to stay this afternoon or come back in the morning? I have appointments so I'll be out of your way."

"It's not quite that easy, Mr. Carver. You have to be a part of this. Otherwise you'll have to call me every time you can't find something because the filing system I've used doesn't make sense to you. And," I ventured, "unless we figure out *why* it got this bad and change your habits, it will happen all over again. We'll have to do some goal setting and prioritizing."

"I don't have the time or need to organize my head, Ms. Smith," he said pragmatically. "Only my shelves. I have an outside meeting this afternoon that shouldn't last more than a couple hours. Right, Jared?" He looked into the bat corner. "I'll just leave you here to begin, Ms. Smith. And please—" he paused at the door "—don't let my secretary in here. She'd have a coronary."

He had that right.

"But I didn't schedule any time for this today…and I need you to be involved…there is no point…" My hands flapped helplessly at my sides. "This isn't my problem to solve alone…"

"It is now," Jared Hamilton said, moving into the light. He looked amused for the very first time, which improved his looks but not the state of my quandary.

"I'll be back at five. That gives you two hours to evaluate my—" Ethan paused and smiled, already showing his relief at having someone to whom to delegate his problem "—situation. I'll talk with you then."

Hamilton sauntered toward the door with his hands in his pockets, looking entirely too entertained. Carver followed him and they disappeared into the outer office. The door whispered closed behind them, leaving me right where I didn't want to be.

As the door closed I heard Hamilton say to Carver, "What are you? Nuts? Craziest thing I've ever heard! What's she going to do for you that you can't do for yourself? You're a smart guy. You can figure this out without an 'organizer.'" He said the word "organizer" the way someone else might say "fleas."

Hah! Being smart and having clutter don't have anything to do with each other. Some of the brightest, most creative people I know can't get their ducks in a row where their possessions are concerned.

I didn't like Jared Hamilton the minute I met him and that comment didn't improve his status with me one bit. A quick prick to my conscience reminded me that I was being judgmental. *Judge not that you not be judged.*

Amen to that.

Immediately dismissing Hamilton, I stared at the stacks of nine-foot-high shelves with my hands resting on my hips, my shoulders squared. Even I felt intimidated and I'm a professional.

I took out the throwaway camera I carry in my purse and did what I always do at the beginning of a job. The "Before" pictures. I assure my clients when I hand them over at the end of a job that I didn't keep negatives and will not use them for blackmailing purposes. Still, I do want them to know just how far they've come in the organizing process. And have something to remind them to never go back there again.

The door opened and I jumped to put my back to the mess and splayed out my arms as if I could even begin to hide this little organizing debacle. But it was Carver again, this time with a boyish grin on his face. "You're saving me big-time, Smith. Even though my friend Jared says you can't do it, I believe you can. I owe you one."

Indeed he did. I spent the rest of the afternoon designing a workable storage system and imagining what it was I was going to demand in payment.

I'm a big believer in categories. Like goes with like. Combs go with brushes, nail polish goes with emery boards and pencils do not go with spoons. Therefore, having to start somewhere, I pulled out an armload of paper, careful not to let the whole stack slide down on me, and started to sort. Prospectuses, financial statements, catalogues filled with golf equipment, personal letters and cartoon books of Calvin and Hobbs were all glommed together in the piles.

I looked around the pristine office and all its beautiful empty floor space. Perfect. Then I went to the door, peeked out and told the secretary that I didn't want to be disturbed under any circumstance and locked the door behind me.

To get in the mood for what I was about to begin, I started to hum. Singing gears me up to dig in to a project that, like this one, is over my head—literally. I make up my own lyrics, usually to something rousing like "Battle Hymn of the Republic."

Mine eyes have seen the messes that have come to me
today
I am trampling out the clutter and the junk where it was
stored
I have given full permission and to the garbage men
implore
Cart this stuff away!
Gory, gory, it's an eyesore,
Gory, gory, it's an eyesore,
Gory, gory it's an eyesore,
The junk is leaving now.

I glanced at the door to make sure there was no way Ethan's
secretary could have found a hidden key and slipped in
unheard by me. If anyone caught me sitting on the floor
singing and shuffling papers like they were playing cards,
they'd probably think they had grounds for commitment. Res-
olutely I began that phase of the project that always dismays
my clients—that It-Will-Look-Even-Worse-Before-It-Looks-
Better stage.

At five-fifteen, when Ethan Carver returned, I had every
square inch of floor space covered with documents, newspaper clippings, letters and articles.

"What on earth?" He stared at the vast sea of paper in dismay.

"No worries," I assured him cheerfully. "Everything on the
floor is sorted by category. Since we didn't have time to talk,
I have some questions for you. I want the files to suit you and
how you think."

"We already have a new filing system. My secretary,
Lorraine, set it up."

I picked up a handful of correspondence. "Then where
would these go?"

Carver studied the papers. "Correspondence is under the

general heading of Code D-yellow. There are sub-files for each correspondent. For example, vendors would be filed under D-4 yellow. Within that vendor file, each correspondent has a sub-sub file. For example, this one——" he waved a paper in front of my nose "——would be filed under Code D-4-12 yellow. Get it?"

I got it all right, but I didn't want it. Ethan must have read my expression.

"Lorraine worked a long time to set this up for me," he said defensively.

"And have you used it?"

"I started the day she finished setting it up."

"And when was the last time you used the system?"

He blushed. "The day she finished setting it up."

"So how's it been working for you?"

He flushed even more deeply. "It's a royal pain in the neck. Stupid. Who has time for that? Besides, I already know what all those papers say. I just need to store them somewhere."

"Okay. So for now we'll make a file called 'Vendors.'" I pointed to a stack of plastic filing crates I'd brought in from my car. "And put it in there. We'll make general categories for everything—golfing information, Calvin and Hobbs, prospectuses, so you have at least a clue where they are and then we'll decide how you actually want to find it if it becomes necessary."

The relief on his face was palpable. For the next two hours Ethan and I crawled around the floor on our hands and knees thinking up logical categories and filling crates. At seven-thirty, I sat straight-legged on the floor with my back propped against his desk and studied him.

He'd lost the jacket and tie, his shoes and his perfectly coiffed hair. He looked happy and rumpled. Relieved of Lorraine's complex filing system, Ethan Carver was a free man.

*I love my job!*

Of course, I felt rumpled, too, and it's not one of my better looks. When my lipstick and blush fade I'm pale as a ghost. I'd tied my hair back with a big red rubber band I'd rescued from an unnecessary file and my blouse was falling out of the waistband of my now snagged and paper-crumb-coated black slacks. Clutter can be a dirty business.

"Well, I guess I'd better get going. I didn't mean for us to be here all night but sometimes, when a client and I are making progress, it's just so much *fun*...." I usually don't say that out loud. Most people don't understand how anyone can get a kick out of diving headfirst into someone else's mess.

He burst out laughing. "Actually, it *was* kind of fun. I haven't been this relaxed or unconstrained in years. How about having dinner with me?"

I blinked. Dinner?

"You don't have to feed me, I'm fine. I often work late...."

"I know I don't have to. I want to—out of appreciation and gratitude. In only a few hours you've given me hope of getting my dirty little secret cleaned up. Now I can open these doors and not have a skeleton in the closet."

"I couldn't..."

"We can grab a pizza just down the block. Frankly, Jared Hamilton and I were supposed to have dinner tonight, but he's got trouble at his office and he cancelled on me. You'd be doing me a favor."

I didn't have any desire to fill in for the tetchy, short-tempered sidekick, but Ethan looked so hopeful.

"Oh, all right."

*Now Jared Hamilton owes me one, too.*

Another gift from my ancestors is the fact that I have the metabolism of a coal furnace. I burn up anything I put into my mouth and never gain a pound. It sounds like a blessing, but it isn't always. I had a boyfriend in college who admitted he could no longer afford me because I ate like a linebacker. I never minded paying my own way, but he had a hang-up about it. Last I heard, he was married to a woman less than five feet tall who eats like a sparrow. *Cheapskate.*

Ethan smiled widely as I finished the last piece of the family-size, deep-dish, with-everything-but-the-kitchen-sink pizza. "I like to see a woman eat."

"Then you must have had a wonderful time tonight. I usually control myself but you kept encouraging me."

He played absently with a piece of silverware still left on the table. "You're an interesting woman, Samantha, and you have a unique job. I assumed I'd be hiring a sort of glorified cleaning lady, but it was very different. No one's ever asked what kind of system works for me or what I consider an efficient office arrangement—even in my own company. It takes someone very clever to comprehend how my mind and office work and then put a plan in place—especially in an afternoon."

"It's remarkable how many people try to live inside someone else's comfort zone and not honor the ways that work best for them."

"So you help people find their 'comfort zones'?" He looked pensive. "Can you help two people with very different 'comfort zones' to get along?"

"It depends. I'm not a miracle worker."

"Interesting, very, very interesting."

He said it thoughtfully, in a way that made me wonder what—or who—he was thinking about.

# Chapter Four

There was already a message on my answering machine from Ethan when I got to work the next morning.

"Hey, Sammi! Great job! Listen, I've got something I want to run by you. Give me a call when you get in."

Theresa gave me a thumbs-up sign as she was walking by my office door.

It had worked out rather well, I thought. Ethan's messy little secret was no longer messy and he was obviously pleased. I could feel a referral or two coming my way.

I dialed his direct number and he picked up on the second ring. "There she is, the woman who put my world in order."

*If only someone I was dating and not a client would say that!*

"I want to talk to you about something, but I want it to stay between us."

"Confidentiality plus," I assured him. "No dirty laundry aired by me, either literally or figuratively."

"I thought so." He took a deep breath, as if he were venturing into dangerous territory. "I asked my friend Jared what he thought of my new professional organizer last night."

*Oh, oh.*

"What did he say?" I asked in my chipper, nothing-will-bother-me voice.

"Do you really want to know?"

"I guess so." Feedback is feedback.

"He told me I was nuts."

"That's no surprise. I saw that written all over his face."

"I thought he, of all people, would understand. He runs his business like a military operation. I've always suspected that he has someone in the back room ironing the creases out of paper." Ethan paused as if he were deciding how much to say. "Or maybe what I'm saying is now past tense. He *ran* his business that way. As he reminded me, it's not that way now."

I remained silent and Ethan continued.

"Normally he's a great guy. You can't find someone with a bigger or gentler heart. He's just angry and frustrated right now. Jared and his sister have a business together. He's having some issues with her, and they've always been very close.

"Anyway, I suggested that he hire an organizational consultant himself. I thought you might be just what he needs."

*What a dandy relationship that would be....*

"What did he say to that?" I asked without enthusiasm.

Ethan is evidently unable to say anything but the honest—and painful—truth.

"That he's not crazy like me. That he needed a personal organizer like he needs another hole in his head. Of course, what he needs has nothing to do with it. He and his sister, Molly, are like night and day, oil and vinegar, yin and yang..."

"There's nothing wrong with two people being dissimilar."

"I told him that and he suggested that *I* take Molly on as a partner and let me know in a month or two how it's going. He regrets taking his sister into his business, and I'd like to help him do something about it."

*Like get him to hire me? Terrific.*

"He's a God-fearing fellow. He told me he'd consulted with the Big Guy about this, but now he tells me I should have talked him out of it."

"Easy as talking water into running upstream?" I asked, getting the bigger picture.

Ethan chuckled. "Of course, if I'd accomplished that, I'd have the credentials for negotiating world peace. Anyway, I wanted you to know that I've been pushing him to give you a call. I think you could help him out."

"Help him out of what? I'm sorry, but this doesn't sound like a job for me. Thank you for the heads-up and the referral, but I'm not a family counselor or a miracle worker."

Despite Ethan's disappointed sigh, I thought, *No thanks. Uh-uh. No, no, no. I want nothing to do with it,* and promptly forgot about any possibility of a job with Jared Hamilton.

# Chapter Five

Two long, grueling days after I'd worked for Ethan Carver, I walked into Theresa's office and dropped into a chair across from her. "Tell me again why I do this for a living."

"Because you love seeing people take charge of their lives, knowing that you've helped them to manage their possessions rather than having their possessions control them. You know that by shifting one's external environment one can shift the internal environment as well. You enjoy interacting with people, you have a talent for making order out of chaos and you like a challenge." Theresa took a deep breath and plunged back into the response she'd memorized for occasions such as this.

"You are also very good at what you do, your clients love you and you make a good living doing it. Today will pass and you will forget all about the fact that…"

She paused for me to fill in the blank.

"…that I spent a day in a kitchen with cabinets that, every time I opened one, would launch china, glasses, pots and pans like Twins' pitchers launch baseballs. And while I was going to the bathroom my client emptied my car of the bags I was taking to Goodwill and dragged them all back inside the house for another look…."

"…and you will live to tell of it another day."

"Thank you. I needed that." I dropped my chin to my chest and rolled my head to one side and then the other in a vain attempt to get the rock-hard knot out of my neck. Theresa is my decompression chamber. If I didn't vent to her, I believe I'd spontaneously combust.

"What else is new?"

"The new storage line arrived and looks great. Mrs. Fulbright called to say that she is ready for 'round two' in the kitchen and she feels emotionally prepared to part with all those lovely plastic disposable plates, forks and spoons she's been washing and reusing. You have two potential clients who want more information. Ben dropped in to tell you that your Aunt Gertie had called. She and her husband are taking fencing classes, but Arthur is a little nervous about Gertie having a sword in her hand. And Wendy called to say that she is at your place cooking dinner. She found a recipe for focaccia that she wants to make from scratch."

I groaned and sank more deeply into the chair. My poor kitchen. Why I haven't sent Wendy Albert, my former college roommate, packing before now is beyond me. We are as far apart on the human continuum as any two individuals can be. Wendy is an actress. Right now she's teaching drama classes, which should be easy for her, since life is drama for Wendy. She was born in the wrong generation. What she really should be is a 1970s hippie, wearing tie-dyed clothing, Birkenstocks and a crumpled cotton skirt made in India, and doing impromptu bits of drama in the park.

Even after all these years, she doesn't have genuine, practical grasp of what I do for a living or how I like to live— neatly. In college, I tried to get her on board with a plan to keep "our" room tidy but it was like talking to a vapor. Every time I said something such as "I'll put my shoes in this closet and you can put your shoes in that one," she disappeared and rematerialized somewhere that neatness wasn't being discussed.

We eventually negotiated a way to live together peaceably. It involved strips of masking tape across the floor and up the walls, marking off which side of the room was Wendy's and which was mine. I dusted and mopped right up to that line and Wendy made hugely messy collages with tiny bits of paper, glitter and dried twigs on her side. She hung them on the wall with masking tape and allowed them to dry and shed on the room all year long. By the end of the second semester, she was sleeping on the floor in a sleeping bag because her bed was buried in books and unfolded clothing and her half of the room looked like a nest put together by sparrows—bits of paper, string, books, underwear and who knew what else. I, meanwhile, had purchased shams and a dust ruffle to match my comforter. It was like being able to see both the light and dark sides of the moon at once.

Of course, I still love her—just as I love Imelda despite the way she desecrated my shoe collection. Like Wendy's, Imelda's excellent traits can't be dismissed lightly. Granted, she's a fashion pup like the Yorkipoo and the schnoodle, but she's also hypoallergenic, she doesn't shed and has very little doggy odor. What dog could be more perfect for me? Besides, it never hurts to *have* to buy new shoes once in a while.

I may be compulsive about neatness but I know where my priorities are—God, family and friends—two- and four-legged—and *then* career. Imelda could eat me out of house and sandal and I'd keep her just the same.

Wendy is highly creative and she is inspired by bedlam and disarray. I've begged her not to cook in my kitchen, but she keeps coming back like a bad rash. Wendy thinks it's her purpose on earth to get me to "loosen up."

I'm already plenty loose.

I'm just loose in a tight sort of way.

"That was great, Wendy," I volunteered. My back was to the kitchen so that I couldn't see the dusting of flour that coated everything from the counters to the ceiling fan. My grandmother has always said that a messy kitchen is a happy kitchen. If that's true, right now my kitchen is giddy with delight.

Wendy studied me with those disconcerting hazel-colored eyes of hers. Whatever color Wendy wears, her eyes take on that color. Tonight, in her baggy, moss-colored cotton sweater, her eyes were a muddy gray green and not easy to read. "Worth the mess?"

"No fair, Wendy. That's a loaded question. You're just trying to make a point. The same point you've been trying to make since we were eighteen."

"Maybe I am. Every time I cook in your kitchen you get these tense little lines—" and she pointed to her forehead "—here. If you aren't careful you'll look old before your time." She picked up a knife and tried to see her own reflection in the blade. "I don't have a single crease."

I turned and eyed my kitchen. "That's because you're a carrier. You make other people frown. You don't frown yourself. You're the Typhoid Mary of frustration."

Every pot and pan I owned was in the sink, Imelda was eating mayonnaise off the floor and the garbage can Wendy had put in the middle of the room for easier access was overflowing, the surplus edging inexorably toward the back door. What's even worse is that Imelda does not digest mayonnaise well.

It took all my self-control to stay in my chair and not run for a mop, a trait that Wendy considers a character flaw or possibly an obsessive-compulsive condition that would be well-served with medication. For years now, she has been trying to train garbage to take itself out. If anyone can do it, Wendy can.

Her earrings jingled as she tipped her head to study me. "It's no surprise that you aren't in a serious relationship, Sammi. There's no one tidy enough for you."

"And what's your excuse?"

Wendy broke into a smile. "I'm too messy. Maybe we're doomed to be the only two people in the world who can stand us."

"Now *that* is a depressing thought." Wendy and I talk about this a lot, especially since many of our friends are already married. It has always been a lighthearted, no worries kind of conversation so I was surprised to realize that this time it hurt.

"What's wrong?" Wendy asked.

"What kind of person *could* live with me, Wendy?"

She raised her eyebrow. "Someone with neatness running in their blood. Someone who lives by the clock, makes lists of everything including when to take a shower and plans his day down to the minute in a perfect leather planner. Oh, yes, and he'd never make a spelling error in his planner, either." She rolled her eyes "Not that *I'd* consider that kind of a guy much of a catch."

It sounded good to me, but I still felt compelled to protest. "I'm not that bad!"

"Maybe not, but you'd need someone even more organized than you in order to be happy. And a Christian, of course, but that almost goes without saying."

Wendy is right about that. My faith is as integral a part of me as my skin or my lungs. I couldn't live without it. But the tidy part…

I thought about Ethan Carver with his perfect office and his dirty little secret hidden behind cupboard doors. Then I considered Ben and his completely scattershot methods. They were fair examples of nice, desirable men. Maybe the man Wendy had described didn't exist.

At that moment my cat Zelda wrapped her way around my ankles to remind me that since Wendy hadn't dropped enough food on the floor for both Imelda and her, I should get busy and feed her. Zelda is a cat but she's never believed it, not even for a moment. Zelda is a diva. She has no self-esteem issues and considers herself to be the finest feline specimen on the planet.

She snaked her way around my ankles, massaging them with her warm body and demanding attention, her distinctive meow sounding like fingernails on a chalkboard. Zelda is very hard to ignore, especially when she's wearing her pink cashmere sweater.

"I see you dressed her for dinner," I commented to Wendy as I scratched Zelda behind one of her large ears and her purring intensified.

Zelda is a sphynx cat, the breed that is normally referred to as "hairless." She isn't bald as a billiard cue like one might assume. Instead, she's covered with a fine down that can be felt but not seen, much like the fuzz on a peach. Sometimes, if I think she's chilly, I put her in one of her little sweaters, most of which I knit or buy in the toy poodle section of the pet store. Wendy gave Zelda the cashmere getup for Christmas and now Zelda's getting particular about what she wears. She has highly developed fashion tastes for something with four legs. She's also insisted on eating her food out of a crystal goblet ever since she saw that cat food commercial on television. And though she hasn't admitted it, I think she has a crush on that big white Persian *and* the hots for one of the cats from the Tidy Cat commercial.

Like Imelda, Zelda is exceedingly special to me, a role model, in fact. Although she is the oddest, most skeletal, bald cat most of my friends have ever seen, Zelda knows she's beautiful. She doesn't *think* it, she *knows* it. It's obvious in the way she moves and in her fearless willingness to take center stage and give herself a bath in a room full of people like a tiny naked yoga instructor doing contortions on my living room floor.

I love the way Zelda knows she's been *created* just the way she is and is perfectly accepting of it. I'm perfect the way God created me, too—He gave me everything I need to fulfill the purpose He has for me, yet sometimes I slink around, embarrassed and think I'm not "good" enough. Zelda is my reminder that if a hairless cat with ears like Dumbo and a personality like Cleopatra can make it, I can, too.

"What about you?" I asked of Wendy, returning to the subject at hand. "What would you need?"

Wendy chewed on her lip while she considered the question. At thirty, Wendy is still occasionally mistaken for a teenager. There is something deceptively innocent and ethereal about her, yet she's anything but ethereal. When Wendy chooses to make an impression, her imprint remains, much like the treads of a bulldozer on soft ground.

"I'd like to say I need someone as messy as me, but I'm afraid that might be asking for trouble."

"I'd say so."

"But I need someone who could understand me."

"Tolerate you, you mean."

Her sweet smile washed over me. "Exactly. You've learned to tolerate me. That means there's hope for me yet."

I forced Wendy to take Imelda for a walk while I did the dishes. She was, after all, the one guilty of making her into a potential doggy time bomb with all that spilled mayo. Maybe it's all the shoe leather she eats that makes Imelda's stomach so touchy. Chips with fiery hot salsa is my downfall but, like Imelda, I pick my poison and eat it anyway.

"Come here, Zelda." I popped the top on a cat food can, piled it into a crystal goblet and put it down on the glittery beaded place mat she loves.

Imperiously she marched toward the goblet, sniffed the contents delicately and considered for a moment if the aroma was satisfying to her sensitive nose and delicate palate. It seemed to be acceptable because she chowed down, purring and gulping like her last meal had been in the 20$^{\text{th}}$ century.

As I scraped and rinsed the dishes, my thoughts returned to Carver Advertising. Or, more accurately, they returned to Jared Hamilton, the storm cloud of a man I'd met there.

I'm not usually hypersensitive, but that man really managed to pet *my* fur the wrong way. Even today his words to Ethan Carver stung. *What are you? Nuts?*

Or so Mr. Know-It-All Hamilton thinks. It's easy to figure out what *others* should do. It's not quite so simple when the problem is in your own backyard. Or with one's own sister.

I found myself scrubbing a dish so hard I was about to remove its painted design. What a waste—that man's gorgeous looks, and a personality like a Brillo pad. For some reason Know-It-All Hamilton really gets on my nerves. Who does he think he is, anyway, snorting and stewing in the elevator, lurking in the shadows at Carver's office and laughing at me?

*He'd* never had desperate messages on his answering machine pleading for help from people who had lost their master's thesis, their promotion, their lease or their job because of the disorder in which they lived and worked. Some of my former clients have me on their emergency call list with their doctor, plumber and the police station.

How dare Jared Hamilton think he knows anything at all about me?

"What's with you?" Wendy asked when she returned with

Imelda. They both looked like they'd been running. "You look like you lost a best friend. But of course you didn't, because that would be me." She gave me a hug and a look of concern.

"No big deal. It was just something someone said, that's all. I think I'm pouting." I hadn't let anyone get under my skin in a long time, but Jared Hamilton had managed it by saying four little words. He'd shaken my confidence without even blinking.

"I'd love to stay and find out what's getting you down," Wendy said, "but I need to get to class. Can I take a rain check on it?"

"Of course. See you later."

And Wendy disappeared through my front door.

Feeling disheartened, I picked up Zelda and nuzzled her. As I took off her cashmere and cuddled her close, she purred until her little body vibrated. Sighing, I took my feline hot-water bottle and my Bible and went to bed.

## Chapter Six

"Be still, my heart!" Theresa swooned into my office on Wednesday, wearing the expression of a bedazzled groupie just having seen her favorite rock star.

"Is that cute FedEx man back?" I asked absently. "I thought he quit to become an underwear model."

"Better."

"What's better than an underwear model who comes bearing cleaning supplies?" I have scoped out vendors who sell hard-to-get products and I must admit that when the FedEx truck pulls up my heart beats a little faster.

"A paying customer who looks even better than the FedEx man!"

"You'd better lay off the lattes for a while." Obviously a case of too many espressos from the machine in the back room.

"No. Truth! Come see for yourself. And he's got a cute friend, too."

Sighing, I stood up and peeked into my minuscule waiting room where a man paced back and forth while another, with rosy cheeks, sat flipping through a magazine. Dark hair with a hint of curl, clean shaven, strong jaw, beautifully shaped nose, eyelashes a woman would trade her jewelry for, a finely cut jacket that caressed broad shoulders and an expression that could freeze hot coffee…. My heart sank.

Theresa jammed her elbow into my side. "I told you so."

She produced a business card with the flair of a magician pulling a rabbit from a hat. "His name is Jared Hamilton. He's president of Hamilton and Hamilton Financial Planners. Ooooh—" Theresa's mouth puckered with anticipation "—maybe he's rich!"

"Don't count your paychecks until they're hatched," I warned. "I've met this guy. I can't imagine why he's here unless he's deluded enough to think he can sell me something."

"A mutual fund pusher? I'll buy some, whatever it is." She prodded me toward the door. "Go find out what he wants."

I hesitated but, unexpectedly, Theresa gave me a helpful shove. I tripped inelegantly into the room, teetered for balance, thrust out my hand and blurted, "Welcome to Clutter Busters. May I help you, Mr. Hamilton? Hello, Ethan."

"You remembered," Hamilton growled.

I smiled more sweetly than I felt. "How could I forget?"

His eyes narrowed as he studied me. I studied him right back. He was even better looking up close, definitely Godiva caliber eye candy. Too bad his flavor is sour ball.

"Samantha Smith, correct?"

"In the flesh." That came out badly. "In person, I mean." I fumbled for something more to say. "I didn't expect to see you here today."

"No, I imagine you didn't. I didn't expect to see me here today, either." He glared at Ethan, who, looking innocent as a cherub, returned his attention to the magazine.

*So it was like that, was it?*

I waited for him to explain, but he didn't. I felt Theresa's eyes boring into my back, so I turned and waved her off. This was awkward enough without an audience.

He shifted from handsomely clad foot to handsomely clad foot as his eyes darted around the office, looking, no doubt, for something out of place.

"You claim you can organize anyone's life, correct?"

"I can help anyone organize their home or office *if* they are motivated, yes. And I can coach someone through the road-blocks that keep them from action."

"Has there ever been a situation you found impossible to handle?" He frowned as he asked the question and a hint of a scowl began to form. Ethan moved the magazine closer to his face. He couldn't possibly be reading since his eyes would be crossed at that distance.

"Not if the client is willing to work with me on setting goals and is motivated to change his or her habits."

"You mean the owner of the mess?"

"Well, yes." I peered into his inscrutable eyes. "Are you in-quiring for yourself?"

Oddly, he flinched. Then he stuck his hands in his trouser pockets as if he didn't know what else to do with them. "Me? Of course not!" he said indignantly.

"Your business or corporation, then?"

"You could say that, I suppose."

Even though he was the one who'd come to me, I felt as though *I* were prying into his personal life. "If not exactly that, why do you want to hire me?"

Unfortunately, people hiring a professional organizer or coach often feel embarrassed about their situation or the fact that they can't handle their predicament alone when, in fact, seeking help is probably the most sensible thing they've ever done.

But Hamilton has an aura of being able to handle anything.

He wears his confidence and capable air like a second skin. Had he come in just to check us out and have a laugh?

"Ethan suggested I talk to you." He squeezed the words through gritted teeth.

*Thanks a bunch for the recommendation,* I thought, with a withering look at Ethan's still-downcast head. *I'll have to send you a plant to show my gratitude—a cactus, maybe, to match your friend's personality.*

I couldn't help myself. "Why?"

"I want you to organize my sister."

"I see." Interesting. I hadn't expected this.

"Do you?" He looked at me oddly.

"I see that you, a third party, are attempting to hire someone as individual as a personal organizer or clutter coach for your sister. Frankly, Mr. Hamilton, that seldom works out satisfactorily. Now if you would send your *sister* in to discuss this…"

He rolled his eyes and made a scornful sound. "Send Molly in? We'd all be gray-haired and senile before she got around to it. No, I just want to hire you. Ethan sang your praises, that's enough for me. I'll let her know that she's getting help."

Then I heard him mutter under his breath, "She certainly needs it."

"I prefer not to work that way," I protested. Oddly, I felt a little dizzy from something in the air—woodsy aftershave? Testosterone?. "Coaching is only effective if the *client* is willing and ready to do what it takes to change."

"You are Molly's final chance, Ms. Smith." His gaze bore into mine hypnotically. He emphasized "final chance."

"I could help her, but it wouldn't last if she isn't involved and willing."

A sigh emanated from somewhere deep and primal inside him, ripping its way painfully to the surface.

His patience was crumbling. *This man has a fuse as short as the wick on a birthday candle.*

What kind of chaos did this sister of his create, anyway? *I've been in this business long enough to never be surprised by anything, but this situation felt different to me.* I glanced at Ethan, but he was still hidden behind the magazine. He was obviously here only for moral support—and not mine.

Hamilton reached for his billfold and pulled a wad of cash from it and put it into my hand. "Here's a partial retainer. I'll write a check for the rest later. Here's the address. When can you be there?"

"We don't even know if I'm the proper coach for you and your sister," I pointed out calmly, although the money was busily making itself at home in my palm.

"Just my sister. Not me. And you'll do fine. Molly can get along with anyone. Just get her straightened out, that's all I ask."

"Let's let Molly decide that." I pushed the money back into his hand. It was warm and strong and his nails were beautifully shaped....

I gave myself a little mental slap on the cheek and continued. "I'm happy to talk with her but I can't just take your money and bully her into something she may not want."

"Let's put it this way, Ms. Smith. My sister has no choice but to shape up. My sister works with me and if she doesn't get her act together soon, I'll have to fire her."

If felt my eyes widen and jaw drop. "You'd fire your own *sister?*" Okay, so the woman had a problem with organization, but she was likely talented in ways that compensated for her to have come this far in business. And if she wasn't totally up to her current job couldn't he just tailor the job more to her skills? I hadn't liked this man yesterday, and he certainly hadn't improved overnight. I don't believe I've ever seen anyone quite so resolute as Hamilton appeared at that moment. His eyes were dark and flat as river stones as he looked at me.

"I would. And I will do it soon. I may have no choice. Think of it this way, Ms. Smith. You are the only thing standing between my sister Molly and unemployment. If you turn this down, you have a heart of stone."

*Me? How did I become responsible all of a sudden? A heart of stone, huh? Well, it takes one to know one!*

I looked at Jared Hamilton with new eyes. Physically luscious, perhaps, but cold as ice in the family relationship department. Disappointment tumbled through me. Where *have* all the good men gone?

After a thankfully brief session over the contract, I left them in my office while I made some copies. Unbeknown to them, the acoustics in my office are such that whatever is said in my office is funneled directly back to where my copy machine sits.

"Calm down, Jared. This will work out," Ethan said.

"That's exactly what Molly said to me when she came to me with her 'brilliant' idea that we should be in business together because her degree in finance and banking background would enhance my financial planning business and bring in new clients."

"In theory, it wasn't a bad idea."

"No? You don't know her like I do. But she wore me down, just like she has a million times since our childhood. She's always been able to twist me around her little finger and this wasn't any different.

"And," Jared continued morosely, "that's when I put my finger on the trigger of the gun that eventually shot me in the foot. I'm just as much to blame as Molly for this fiasco. I, at least, should have known better."

I heard him shifting in his chair. "I just can't quit thinking of Molly as a little girl. She depended on me to get her out of every jam she was in—and there were many."

"But you aren't going to bail her out this time," Ethan said softly.

"Not out of this. It's too big. Too important."

"Then it's a good thing we came here, Jared. Sammi can help."

"It says 'Clutter Busters' on the door, Ethan. Not 'Miracle Worker.' I've never felt so foolish in my life," Jared growled. "This isn't going to work, and you know it."

"I know nothing of the kind. She helped me enormously. I plan to use her again. She gives seminars. I'm bringing her in to speak to every department." Ethan paused before adding, "Besides, she's great-looking. That alone should be of interest to you."

"I don't have time for looking. I've got my plate full and you know it."

Ethan whistled under his breath. "You? With no time to notice women? This is even more serious than I thought."

I cleared my throat as a warning and reentered the room.

When we were done, Jared bolted out the door of Clutter Busters and into the street. I watched him go. He looked to the right and to the left almost as if he were afraid to be caught coming out of such a questionable establishment as my office. You'd have thought he was leaving a bordello or bank heist.

"So you're really going to do it?" Theresa sat on the edge of my desk swinging one leg and looking avidly curious. "You're going to allow yourself to be hired by this guy to help his sister?"

"Of course not. I left the contract empty for his sister to fill out if *she* wants to hire me." I studied my list of supplies to make sure I had everything I'd need if I actually took this

assignment—markers, label maker, empty files, see-through
containers, garbage bags, catalogues of shelf organizers and
office supplies. "I'm simply going to meet the sister. Together
*we* will decide if she'd like me to work with her."

"It doesn't sound to me like she has much say in the
matter." Theresa snapped her gum. "Fired by her own brother
from her own company. Wicked. I wonder what she did to
deserve this."

My thoughts exactly. I hadn't even met the woman I was
supposed to assist and I was already enraged at the way she
was being treated. In my family, we went to the mat for one
another. I couldn't imagine either of my brothers doing
anything like this to me. I know what it is to be the adored
little sister—it doesn't involve being kicked out of a family
business. What kind of jerk was this Hamilton guy, anyway?
I'm even annoyed with myself for thinking he was good-
looking now that I know what he's up to. I usually have better
taste than that.

"Next step, his royal highness and the command perfor-
mance," I muttered.

I was early, I realized as I drove south on France Avenue.
Hamilton's office wasn't far from Benjamin's home. Impulsively, I turned the corner and headed for Ben's place. He
usually works at home on Thursdays and since I didn't want to
arrive too early at Hamilton and Hamilton, it was a logical stop.

Ben's place is a sophisticated junkyard as far as I'm concerned. Sophisticated because everything he collects involves
circuitry, wires, computer chips and other scientific-looking
litter. He also amasses huge numbers of books with titles so dull
and dry that I'm stumped as to where he finds them all. It's
probable that someone in his family wrote them. For example,
until I met Ben, I never knew how many kinds of physics there

were—quantum, classical, conceptual, particle, statistical, thermal, nuclear—the exhilarating list goes on and on.

Ben's thinking of naming the book he's writing *Aristotle, Einstein, Murphy's Law and Little Old Me.* I'm sure it will read like a thriller compared to the others on his shelf. Meanwhile his house is still a junkyard. Ben can wire together an electric razor and a vacuum cleaner and have the thing clean the carpets and turn them from shag into plush at the same time but he can't find a way to corral wire nuts, microchips or the tiny scraps of paper on which ideas for brilliant new inventions are written. Ben would have invented a cure for the common cold by now if only he could find the deposit slip on which he wrote the idea when it first came to him.

"Hey!" I called from the doorway. "Anybody here?"

"Just us mice." Ben appeared from his bedroom with a book under one arm. He was wearing gray sweatpants, a "Scientists Make Connections" T-shirt and a hairdo created by a tornado. "What are you doing here?"

"I'm on my way to meet a client and I thought I'd stop to say hello."

"Is she cute?" Ben inquired.

"No date for this weekend, huh?"

"Just thought I'd ask. Want coffee?" Ben looked around dazedly as if he were trying to remember where he had put the coffeepot. "I've also got chocolate."

Ben knows me too well.

"Maybe some for later. I can't stay."

He turned around and headed for the kitchen. Shortly he came back with a bag of chocolate chips, an Oreo and a large package of assorted miniature candy bars. "What's your fancy?"

"Candy bars, I think."

He thrust the entire bag into my hands. "Enjoy."

"I can't take all your candy."

"You won't. I'm working late all of next week so I bought five bags to tide me over until I can get dinner."

"You should weigh four hundred pounds."

He face broke into a boyish grin. "And I have trouble staying at one eighty."

"I know women who'd give anything for your metabolism."

His eyes shifted from side to side. "That reminds me. I was going to talk to my brother about my ideas on increasing the metabolic rate in humans. Do you have a deposit slip in your purse? I need to write this down…."

After leaving Ben's house, I was sure that nothing else in the way of disorganization could surprise me.

I should have been warned, however, that I was up for something special by the "Quarantined" sign on one of the doors beyond Hamilton and Hamilton's elegant reception area and front office. If that didn't do it, the skull and cross-bones right next to it should have.

## Chapter Seven

The receptionist followed my gaze and shuddered slightly. "Ms. Hamilton has a quirky sense of humor. Pay no attention."

It was difficult not to pay attention, considering the skull and crossbones were neon orange.

Before I could inquire further, Jared Hamilton strode out of another office on the far side of the reception area.

He was as imposing and handsome as the last time we'd met, maybe even more so in his own environment. Was that a Bible, I wondered, on the credenza behind the desk? This office, other than the quarantine sign and skull and crossbones, was exactly how I'd imagined it might be, satisfyingly perfect—especially with the Bible in it.

He seemed to read my mind and glanced at the offending door. A grimace marred his face for an instant. Then it became smooth and unreadable again.

Granted, the door to what was obviously his sister's office was idiosyncratic, but there was no law against that. My biggest challenge in this business is being nonjudgmental. I'm flexing that muscle all the time. God's helping me. It's a good thing He's patient because I'm not His best student in this area. Some people can only think straight when there's no mess around them. Others are more creative in chaos. I'm one of the former and remind myself often that one isn't better than the other, just different. I think people are born with certain inclinations that lean one way or the other.

When my mother read *Snow White and the Seven Dwarfs* to me when I was a child, I always wondered why Snow White wanted all those dwarfs like Sleepy, Grumpy and Dopey around. If it were me, I remember thinking, I'd just have one—Spotless.

I'm teaching myself to relax in a mess. Sometimes I consciously drop my junk mail on the floor and don't pick it up all day—just to see how long I can stand it. I practice leaving dishes in my sink and not making my bed in the morning immediately upon getting up. I suffer, but I am determined not to become annoying about cleanliness. My grandmother never greeted me at her door without a paper towel in hand to wipe away any dust or mud that might have clung to my shoes. She insisted I eat my cookies over a plate at the kitchen table and acted as though spilling cookie crumbs on the floor was a premeditated criminal act, like blowing up Fort Knox.

"You are right on time," Jared said approvingly, and I felt as if I'd just been patted on the head. Hamilton *is* actually physically capable of patting me on the head, being taller than me by at least five or six inches. That, at least, is a pleasant change.

Maybe there isn't an overabundance of short men in the world, but some days it feels that way to me. Still, I've never let it scare me out of my high heels and into flats. If God's got someone for me in my size, he'll be along when the time is right.

"Please, come into my office." He gestured toward his door. Beyond it was a room with a vast mahogany desk, a black leather chair and so many windows that for a moment I thought the office might be open to the elements. The bookcases along the side walls were ordered and tidy, each book carefully positioned with its spine even with the front of the shelf.

"Very nice," I commented as my heart did cartwheels. This place was perfect! Even I couldn't dream of more. I took the chair Hamilton offered me. A gentleman, a tidy gentleman. Finally, something we had in common. Things were looking up.

"Thank you." He adjusted his pen so it lined up with the edge of his calendar.

"That's your sister's office across the hall, I take it."

He winced. "Yes. Molly will join us shortly. It seems she's caught in traffic."

"It was bad today," I commiserated. "Roadwork."

"Not traffic on the street, in the coffee shop. Molly can make an ordeal out of anything. She called to say that her 'half-caf, half-decaf sugar-free Irish crème latte' had arrived as a decaf vanilla cappuccino or something like that. No doubt she wasn't paying attention when she ordered." He ran his finger around the inside of his pristine white shirt as if he were a living illustration of the term "hot under the collar."

For once, I had no idea what to say in response. It was a much more creative excuse than "the dog ate my homework."

"Maybe it's for the best. I didn't do a good job of explaining exactly *why* I want you to work with my sister. Perhaps I could clarify myself."

*I doubt it, but you can try.*

"Just remember that it is *her* decision whether she wants to work with me or not," I pointed out. "She is the one who will ultimately have to make the changes and do the work. No matter how much you want help for her, I can't be on retainer for life."

*Although you're cute enough for me to consider it...* said a naughty but familiar little voice in my head. It was as if Wendy were sitting on my shoulder ready and willing to do a play-by-play of the action. Granted, Hamilton was handsome, but he was obviously a misogynist. Wendy has no common sense whatsoever so I banished her from my thoughts.

Shaking off impending schizophrenia and brushing the shoulder of my suit as if to sweep troubling thoughts—and Wendy—off my back, I lifted my chin. "And if she doesn't want to be helped, I'd be wasting your time and mine to try."

He looked tired, as if just thinking about his sister was a chore. For the first time I noticed a hint of vulnerability in his eyes. I was suddenly insatiably curious and wanted to meet Molly myself and figure out how she could so thoroughly bollix up this obviously competent man's life. I felt a twinge of admiration for a personality that strong. She must be quite a woman.

He took the chair behind the desk, leaned back in it and tented his fingers beneath his chin. He could have been posing for a portrait of the quintessential CEO hatching new ideas for the company.

"Maybe a little history is in order," he said finally, as though telling it would be no simpler than having one's appendix removed through one's nostrils.

"Please."

"I'm seven and a half years older than my sister, who is thirty-one. My parents are highly successful in their own right. Mother is an educator. She's an administrator for a large school district. My father is a banker who has turned a small, privately owned bank into a thriving lending center."

"Impressive."

"It's in part due to their abilities to organize and delegate," Jared said. "They are both brilliant in that area."

"As are you, I imagine."

He nodded. "Unfortunately, Molly didn't get the gift."

I was beginning to see a picture come into focus.

"I'm a great deal like my parents," Jared said frankly. "Ambitious, goal-oriented and focused. Even as a child, I knew that someday I wanted to create my own business. I built Hamilton Financial from the ground up."

"I thought it was Hamilton *and Hamilton.*"

He frowned. "Two years ago, my sister came to me with the idea that she join my company. Molly is smart as a whip when she chooses to be. She has a degree in finance but has worked only in tightly structured banking systems. I was considering taking on a partner anyway and I thought, despite my reservations, I could make it work."

Now we were at the meat of the story. "'Reservations'?"

His eyes glazed and I thought for a moment I'd lost him but he rallied and continued. "Molly and my mother have never seen eye-to-eye about my mother's insistence on order and method. Mother thinks that there should be a system for everything."

I knew by the way he said it that he agreed wholeheartedly.

"But your sister works on the theory that everything will sort itself out in the end?" I guessed. I can't even remember how many times I've heard this story.

He raised an eyebrow in surprise. "You might say that."

"She accuses the entire family of being nagging, anal retentive, nitpicking and overly fussy."

"Apparently you've been at our family dinners."

"And she's made it her life's duty to rebel against everything your parents tried to teach her?"

"That's how it appears, especially where system, structure, organization and orderliness are concerned." He gave a small, rueful laugh. "Of course, you won't get Molly to admit that. She simply says she has to be true to herself and she *can't* make sense of her stuff so there's no use trying. Hence, the quarantine sign on her office door."

"She must have a good sense of humor to have put it there."

"I put it there," Jared said grimly, no humor in his voice whatsoever.

He must have seen my shocked expression. I quickly gathered my face into a smooth, professional appearance. Cool as a cucumber, that was the impression I liked to portray.

"And I have no more tolerance for Molly's messes, especially not when they involve my business and my financial future."

This was a new twist.

"Molly's carelessness and her 'it will all work out' attitude recently cost the company two influential clients whose portfolios were mismanaged due to my sister's disorganization. She didn't get the correct information into her files. She no doubt laid important material on her desk and buried it under an accumulation of papers, junk mail and Big Mac wrappers. We lost two clients we couldn't afford to lose."

Hamilton's eyes were icy and his voice hard as he concluded, "Either you get my sister shaped up or I'll ship her out, Ms. Smith. I'm sorry it's come to this but I don't care anymore what it will do to our relationship or our family. I've spent my life bailing her out and now she's forced me to resign as her keeper."

There was an inexplicable sadness in his eyes. Then he steeled himself and continued. "I wish you all the success in the world, because I'm afraid that without this business, her lifestyle and our relationship will alter radically."

Shocked, I started to stammer "But you can't..." *Oh, but he could.* "What about your parents?"

His eyes turned cold. "Washed their hands of her messes long ago. No one knows what to do with her. We all love her, but Molly is yours now. Good luck." Then he pushed a check across the desk to me.

I stared at the handsome, chiseled face and the determined set of his jaw. He wasn't kidding. Suddenly this helpful, hopeful little business of mine was the only thing between a woman and financial doom.

Then the goofy neon skull and crossbones flickered into my mind. Somebody in this mess had a sense of humor. And, although I believed Jared Hamilton would fire his sister without compunction, he *was* willing to put out good money to stop it from happening first.

It was a start, at least.

We stared at each other across his massive desk until he made a vain attempt to roll the tension out of his shoulders, and pulled his fingers through his dark hair in a gesture of frustration. I could tell that he felt at least partially to blame for Molly's carelessness and inattention to detail. He'd admitted that he'd doted on her from the day she came home from the hospital, taking the blame for any childhood infractions she might commit and protecting her from anyone who tried to curb her free-spirited tendencies. He'd adored his little sister and it nearly killed him to make her unhappy, and now...

"I only hope it isn't too late to pull Molly together."

We both started when the telephone rang.

"It's Molly, sir. Shall I put her through?" his secretary said.

"I suppose that now is as good a time as any."

Although he didn't have the speakerphone on, I could make up much of what his sister was saying.

"Jared, it's Mol. Listen, I'm sorry I couldn't make it to the meeting. I know you haven't wanted to talk to me before now. I understand that you needed time to cool off, but you and I have never gone this long being upset with each other." Molly's voice choked. "I know I blew it! I realize that I didn't live up to your expectations, but you know me, I have a little trouble with organization. It seems so unimportant in the scheme of things...."

"You call what happened 'unimportant'?"

"You offered me another chance, Jared, and I'm taking it. It won't happen again, you'll see."

"You're right, Molly, it won't happen again. I'll make sure of it. You're going to need help. Your good intentions haven't gotten you anywhere in the past. It's time to take action."

"Anything, Jared. Just tell me what I need to do. I won't disappoint you again. I couldn't bear it."

"I've hired someone to work with you on these issues. Her name is Samantha Smith. Ethan believes that she can help you."

"I love you, Jared. You are so good to me. I'll be a trouper, I promise."

"One chance to change," he finally said through gritted teeth. "*One*. And then you're out, Molly. It's as you've often pointed out, we aren't brother and sister in this, we're business partners, and if you don't get your act together there will be a hostile takeover very soon."


"What kind of guy would throw his sister out onto the street? And you think this guy is a Christian?" Theresa chewed and snapped her gum so loud and fast that it sounded like she was popping bubbles in plastic packing material. "What a jerk!"

"She was irresponsible, Theresa," I ventured. "We don't know enough about the situation to draw any conclusions. She does need to be accountable for her own actions, just like the rest of us."

"Yes, but at what cost? She's his sister, after all!" Her hands, bloodred nails and all, clenched into fists. "If he comes in here again, I think I'll pop him!"

"Then you and Molly can look for jobs together," I said calmly. Mrs. Fulbright and her excess plastic seemed more and more like a walk in the park.

Theresa suddenly locked her attention on me and said, "You're a Christian. What does the Bible say about this?"

A relatively new Christian, she's always asking me what the Bible says about everyday issues.

"There are all sorts of sibling imbroglios in Scripture—Esau and Jacob, Cain and Abel, Joseph and his brothers—but none that addresses anything quite like this." I tried to imagine anyone quibbling over disarray in the pasture or unfilled parchments lying around in the tent library, and came up short.

"I thought you said the Bible had something to say about everything."

"Yes, I did say that. And I believe it's true."

"I'll be waiting to hear what it is."

*Okay, Lord. I know You are relevant for every age and every question. What about this one?*

"He's going to fire her over something as minor as a messy desk?" Wendy said, shocked. "Why did you say you'd work for him?"

"I didn't say I would work for *him*. And I don't think it's as simple as all that."

"Then why do you have that?" Wendy pointed at the check lying on her kitchen table. We were drinking chai and eating crackers with cheese from a can after taking my dog for a walk. Imelda pranced by with the mate to the shoe she'd eaten yesterday and had refused to relinquish when we'd left home, and I didn't have the energy to stop her. Soon there were gnawing sounds coming from beneath my chair. Every once in a while she paused to burp.

My mind went to the little shoe cannibal beneath me. It doesn't make sense, I suppose, for someone as meticulous as me to have a dog with a shoe fetish like Imelda's, but I do have to take some responsibility in the matter. My shoes now reside in shoe racks that hang in my closet, off the floor and out of Imelda's reach.

I also remember thinking Imelda was cute the first time she shredded an old slipper, shaking her head and growling at it as if she'd been on safari and it were big game. I'd initially encouraged the problem from which I now suffered. Wasn't it, in part, my doing? I didn't put an end to the behavior when it started to happen. Now I'm living with the fruits of my laziness.

Theresa has a theory about pets and children—if you can't train them, outsmart them. Unless, like Imelda, they outsmart you first. Maybe something like this applied in Jared and Molly's case?

"I'm doing it for his sister's sake," I said, glancing back at the check in question. "And I'll be working with Molly, not her brother. She agreed without hesitation."

What I didn't admit to Wendy was that I could feel tiny twinges of Jared's pain. I don't necessarily like the man, nor do I approve of him firing his own sister. I'm not pleased that he is so firm in his decision to do it, but I know how it is to be sucked into the vortex of someone else's mess.

I looked around Wendy's apartment and suppressed a sigh. She'd been creating homemade paper, and the place looked like hordes of mice had chewed the entire place to shreds. Or was it locusts? It's so hard to tell which creepy-crawly critter Wendy imitates best.

"So you didn't get to meet the sister?" Wendy sat cross-legged in front of her fireplace, the one that she hadn't been able to light in nearly a year because she stored unread magazines in it.

"No. Apparently one thing led to another in the coffee shop, and last I heard before I left Hamilton's office was that she'd left her purse on the counter and someone had walked off with it. She was filing a report with the police so I suggested we meet on a better day."

"What did her brother say to that?"

"That there is no 'better day.' He said every day is like this with Molly."

"What have I gotten myself into, Zelda?" She perched on the edge of the bathtub watching me remove my makeup. She tilted her head to one side as if considering her answer and the rhinestones in her collar sparkled in the light.

Zelda is a girlie cat. In addition to cashmere and silk, she adores wearing little bejeweled collars and can sit for hours in front of my full-length mirror, turning her head and watching the glints of light reflecting from the fake diamonds. You'd think a hairless cat would feel embarrassed by her lack of the one thing most cats share in common—fur—but not Zelda. She knows it makes her special to be nude and it's her job to maximize on it.

I'd read about hairless cats but never expected to see—or own—one until Ben came to my house one night with a cloth pet carrier, a litter box and a big grin.

"She's perfect for you, Sammi." He thrust out the carrier for my inspection. "No shedding. Isn't it great?"

Great wasn't exactly what I'd thought as I'd peered into the carrier and a little wrinkled Yodalike face peered back. At the time I couldn't think of a single benefit to having a naked cat in the house, no matter how exotic or unique it might be.

Since then I've changed my mind. Zelda, with her wrinkled little forehead and intelligent eyes, is the best listener I've ever met. She doesn't shed, is meticulous in the litter box and, although I don't admit it to just anyone, a great bed partner. Sleeping with Zelda is like sleeping with a warm football. Imagine pigskin heated up, supple and purring, and you've got Zelda.

I opened my arms and she jumped in. Her hot-to-the-touch

body comforted me. Here I was, in five-year-old pajamas, wearing my retainer, manless and conflicted about my work.

"Maybe I'm too fussy, Zelda," I murmured. She kneaded my arm with her claws and nudged her nose under my chin, her way of telling me it was time to go to bed and that I'd feel better about everything in the morning.

As I fell into a restless sleep and was haunted all night with nightmares, I dreamed that everyone in my life, both male and female—including Jared Hamilton and Ethan Carver and especially Jared's sister, Molly—had grown fur and were sitting on my couch shedding as Wendy fed them peanuts and encouraged them to drop the shells on my newly vacuumed floor.

# *Chapter Eight*

This is how I use the second law of thermodynamics (Energy flows from being concentrated in a single place to becoming diffused, dispersed and spread out. Or, anything left to itself tends toward disorganization.) in my work: Contained materials or objects will always spread out once they are no longer contained. They will, however, *never* pick themselves up and put themselves away. Imagine picking up a basket full of dirty clothes and turning it over. The clothes will fall to the floor and cover the carpet. They will not, however, leap off the floor and back into the basket. Once a snowball starts rolling down a mountainside and picking up more snow, left to its own devices, it will likely cause an avalanche.

It's the same with possessions, papers and the like. If you don't keep your stuff contained in files, containers or drawers, it's going to spread out all over your place and, once the spreading begins, it's really hard to get it all contained again. Think about that snowball, that hill and that impending avalanche—or the fact that no matter how hard you try, you cannot teach laundry to get into a basket by itself.

Granted, although our stuff is just itching to get loose and act on its tendency to disperse, we can prevent it from happening. And that's where I come in. I'm the one standing between my clients and chaos because I've got the tips and tools for impeding that clutter spread.

This might not satisfy a scientist, but it's good enough for me.


Feeling a little cocky that I even know what the second law of thermodynamics is, I made my way to Molly Hamilton's house on Friday with an attitude just waiting to be humbled.

Her brother had to be exaggerating about her inability to keep things in order. We could probably settle this in a few sessions and I would be the one responsible for reuniting sister and brother and healing the rift between them. The idea appealed to the good Samaritan in me. Then I could get on with the job of spending the healthy check Hamilton had given me.

*Pride goes before destruction, and a haughty spirit before a fall.*

I was already mentally purchasing Jimmy Choos and a new file cabinet in cherry-red when I rang the doorbell of the attractive town house located in a very trendy part of the city. Whatever Molly was doing wrong, she must also be doing something right. One can't afford to live in this part of town if they are a continual goof-up.

Or so I thought.

"Who is it?" A woman's timid voice came from behind the door.

"Samantha Smith with Clutter Busters."

The door flew open and I was jerked inside so quickly that I nearly left my shoes on the front porch. The door slammed shut behind me. I was greeted by an attractive woman in a business suit. She wore a smile of relief on her face.

"Sorry about dragging you in like that, but I'm not keen on opening my door for the neighbors to peek in. They're retired and have designated me as their live entertainment when there's nothing on television." Molly looked a little shamed. "If my foyer looked better, I wouldn't mind, but as it is…"

Then I looked past her and into her home.

"I see what you mean."

There was a canoe leaning against one wall, a bicycle against the other, tennis rackets spouting out of an umbrella stand, umbrellas hanging from the upper door jamb like icicles after a storm, athletic clothes and the duffel bags they should have been in, tennis shoes, unread newspapers, a guitar and seven boxes of Girl Scout cookies filling what might once have been a very pretty area. The canoe took up most of the space and blocked the main portion of the living area from view but I could still see slippery mountains of magazines, baskets of unfolded laundry and teetering stacks of CDs and tapes beyond.

"My brother used to say I needed a bomb-sniffing dog to get around in here," Molly admitted cheerfully. "But now he's changed his mind. He's afraid a dog loose in here would never find its way out again." She stopped talking to stare at me. "Jared is right—you *are* pretty!"

That took me aback for a moment but once it sunk in, I felt a ripple of pleasure flow through me. Though I don't even like Molly's infuriating brother, I couldn't help being flattered.

Before I could open my mouth, however, Molly continued. "He's terribly angry with me right now. I've disappointed him. It's just that it's impossible for me to be meticulous like him. Totally impossible."

"A self-fulfilling prophecy?" I murmured to myself.

Molly heard me. "Right. You want me to *think* this place into order?"

My mind raced as I studied her. She was slender and pretty in a soft, delicate way. Her light brown hair framed her face in loose curls and her cheeks and lips were naturally rosy. Likeable. That's the best word that I could use to describe Molly. There was something about her that made her easily and instantaneously likeable. She had none of the sharp edges or disapproving expressions that her brother had. If Jared was a rabid bat, Molly was a fluffy baby bunny.

Looking around the room before me and then remembering Jared's pristine environment made me wonder if there were any similarities whatsoever between the two.

"Would you like to come into what my brother calls 'Tornado Alley'?" She stepped over one of the canoe's oars and into the living room.

With efficiency born of much practice, Molly tossed throw pillows, afghans, workout clothing, books and pizza boxes off the couch onto the floor and offered me a seat.

"I had a cleaning lady for a while," she said cheerfully, "but she fired me. She said it was the first time she'd ever had to do that. But she told me that if I ever got the place under control, she'd consider coming back. Wasn't that nice of her?"

I couldn't help but stare at this personable, pretty young woman who, by all accounts, could create chaos faster than anyone—even a professional—could clean up.

"You're rather upbeat about it."

Unexpectedly, her hazel-colored eyes clouded with tears. "I detest it, Ms. Smith."

"Call me Sammi."

"Sammi, I loathe the fact that I'm isolating myself. I can't have my friends into my house because they'd be shocked. I despise it that none of my family wants to come here to visit. And I can't stand it that my only brother thinks I'm somehow doing this to spite him and my parents!"

She sat down on the corner of a chair housing a pair of eight-pound weights, a fishing tackle box, a wad of towels and a stack of unopened mail. "And I am so disgusted with myself for not being able to figure out what to do about it! What's wrong with me?"

"Nothing is 'wrong' with *you*. God created you. Your habits need a little work, that's all. This is doable. We'll figure something out."

I saw relief spread across her features like sunlight over shade.

"And my brother won't hate me anymore?"

"'Hate' is a strong word."

"You're right. Jared couldn't hate me even though he has every reason to do so. He wouldn't even know how. Besides, he's a Christian. That's what makes him so patient with me, I'm sure of it."

I pondered her convoluted statement. "I can't imagine anyone not succumbing to your charm," I assured her.

She looked at me with an odd, evaluating expression. "Then you don't understand what's been going on between me and my brother lately."

I didn't, but that overheard conversation in my office had sent up a few red flags.

I left Molly Hamilton's house with a vague sense of foreboding.

What am I getting myself into? I wondered as I slipped into the front seat of my car. I leaned wearily against the headrest. I had to think. There were dynamics here I didn't understand. Molly needed me and had agreed to work with me but her brother Jared was the one footing the bill. Who was the client here, really? That, I knew, would have to be very clear before I cashed his check.

I returned to my office to find Wendy sitting at Theresa's desk helping her put printed labels on an advertising flyer and laughing heartily at something. When I walked in, Wendy straightened to attention and I had a sense that if she'd dared, she would have saluted.

"At ease, Wendy."

She grinned. "Sorry. So how did the skirmish go?"

"I'm not captain of the Sanitation Army, you know."

"How quickly I forget."

If Wendy isn't good for anything else, she's great at pricking my ego and deflating it to size.

I dropped into the chair across from her. "Jared Hamilton is right. His sister needs me."

"So what's the problem, then?"

"I'd rather that she'd called me herself, I suppose. Even though she seems excited, even enthusiastic about this, I'm not crazy about having a middleman to answer to."

"So don't answer," Wendy said cheerily. "You make everything too hard, Sammi. That's why Theresa and I did some work for you. We're helping you out."

Wendy and Theresa collaborating in my behalf gives me a cold chill. That was like "helping" an Eskimo build an igloo by offering to hold a hair dryer on his work.

Before I could say anything, Theresa thrust a piece of paper in front of me. "Here. We worked out a quiz for you to give your clients. If they answer 'yes' to three or more questions, they need to hire you."

Clutter Busters Suitability Quiz—If Your Life Isn't Cluttered, You Don't Need Busting!

1. Do you say to yourself "If I can't make it all perfect then what's the use of doing it at all?"
2. Do you have luggage, boxes, furniture or your birdcage stored in your bathtub or shower?
3. Do you have magazines that are at least three years old somewhere in your house, waiting to be read?

4. Do you sleep on top of your bedspread rather than crawling between the sheets because you'll just have to make it again in the morning anyway?

5. Have you given up folding your laundry because you'll just be using the clothes again tomorrow?

6. Do your friends insist on *not* coming to your home?

7. Have you had to look in the refrigerator to find your nail polish, shoes, hairspray or parakeet?

8. Do you have good intentions and absolutely no follow-through?

9. Is there always something late, lost, overdue, misplaced, outdated, moldy or unidentifiable in your home?

"You've got to admit. It will make them think."

It certainly made *me* think. I realized that Molly Hamilton could answer yes to every single question.

# Chapter Nine

My idea of good working conditions does not involve an irate brother hovering around, breathing steam down the neck of my client. But, by the look of things, that is Jared Hamilton's plan. I tried to tactfully dissuade him but it didn't work.

"You don't have to stay, Mr. Hamilton. Molly and I will get along beautifully. It's Monday morning. I'm sure you must have dozens of things to take care of at your office."

He didn't bite. Instead he appeared to dig his heels in a little deeper. "I'm here for the duration" was written all over his face.

I glanced around the room and my gaze fell on a family picture. Jared and what were obviously his parents stared pleasantly out of the frame, he and his father in dark suits, his mother in a tailored navy dress, her hair done to perfection and the smile on her face serene. And then there was Molly.

Molly, noticing what I was looking at, told me the story.

"What a day that was! I was late for our family picture. I'd thought I'd have time to launder the dress I planned to wear, but—silly me—I didn't read the tag or think about the fact it contained wool. I discovered the hard way that I should have taken it to the dry cleaners. So I just wore something from my closet that was clean. It worked out fine, though, don't you think?"

What was clean in her closet was a bright turquoise sweater covered with beads in the design of a parrot. In contrast with the rest of her well-dressed family, the photo looked less like a family picture and more like a snapshot of three Supreme Court Justices and Dolly Parton.

I glanced around her living room and made a mental note to have her clear places for us to sit down. The places she'd cleared last time had already disappeared.

Molly was admiring the colored laundry baskets I'd brought to sort items into. "By the way, call my brother Jared, otherwise I won't know who you're taking about." She, who might have been angry or bitter about her brother's heavy-handedness, was happy and chirpy as a bird in spring. Jared, however, resembled a fractious vulture that hadn't seen road-kill in a very long time.

"Jared, then. Molly and I will be just fine sorting through these—" I turned to look at the breathtaking display of clothing, books, blankets, DVDs, dishes, food cartons, tapes, art supplies, ski equipment and papers decorating her living room "—for quite some time."

"No, I'll stay." His brows furrowed. "You may find something important that I need in this mess."

I turned to Molly for direction.

Molly sighed. "I'm afraid he's right, Sammi, I have lost a few things that we really do have to find…my birth certificate, for one. And an agreement between Hamilton and Hamilton and another company that's necessary to move ahead with some business Jared is working on."

"And you brought it here?"

Molly brightened. "Now *that* much I remember. I was

planning to look it over one evening." She looked around the room. "I just don't know where I could have put it."

Was that what Jared was so angry about that he'd brought me in to help his sister restore order to her life? She'd lost something vital to the company? It would explain some of his temper. Whatever it was, it had to be important, or he wouldn't be insisting on overseeing this whole process like Sherlock Holmes with a magnifying glass in hand.

"Books in the red basket, magazines and newspapers in the blue, sporting equipment in the green, pizza boxes in the trash can…" Molly was reiterating what I'd told her, making a game out of the sorting. "Laundry in the white and…where did you say the loose papers should go?"

Jared pounced on the stack of papers she held in her hand. "I'll take those."

"And all papers to Darth Vader, scourge of the messy."

We were able to keep Jared out of the picture most of the morning by feeding him stray papers and mail to sort. By noon, other than the heaping laundry baskets lined along the walls and seven huge trash bags bulging at the seams, the living and dining spaces revealed actual flooring and flat surfaces.

"I love it!" Molly squealed, as if I were a designer on the Home and Garden channel and she were a happy home owner looking at her newly decorated digs. "I'd forgotten how nice it is in here." She studied the room. "I thought my carpet was a different color, too. I'm going to keep it this way from now on."

I heard a strangled cough from the kitchen where Jared had taken a post to do his sorting, but, to his credit, he didn't voice what he was thinking.

Molly, reminded that he was there, went to him and threw her arms around him. "This was a great idea, Jared. Thank you."

I saw a faint flicker of amusement and affection in his expression before his default expression of stern disapproval returned. "You're welcome, Molly, but we aren't done yet. You know what I said…"

"Oh, you won't have to fire me now, Jared. I know you won't. I'm trying very hard. Can't you tell?"

I, an outside observer watching the pair from a distance, was not so sure.

I'd never before realized how annoying a perfectionist could be. Did people think of me the thoughts I was thinking about Jared Hamilton?

He stood up and came with Molly back to the living room, pausing to straighten a stack of books on the coffee table.

"Don't *do* that," I said, firmly directing his hands away from the books. "They'll be fine."

"They'll fall over and make another mess."

"They'll be fine," I insisted, although I knew that they were likely to tumble over for me to pick up again. If I felt a little rebellious at being told how to do my work, I could only imagine what Molly had put up with.

"You two go to lunch," Molly instructed before our conversation could escalate. "I'm going to stay here and sit in my beautiful, tidy house."

"You aren't done for the day, are you?" Jared said with a frown. "You've barely scratched the surface."

Molly's eyes had the glazed, unfocused look of the emotionally exhausted. To Jared, the morning had been about sorting through junk. To Molly, it had been a hike up an emotional Mount Everest.

"She needs a break. Besides, you have homework, right, Molly?"

She looked a little stricken, but nodded. "Get boxes, label them 'Give Away,' 'Throw Away' and 'Store.' Sort through all this stuff and, if I don't love it or use it, put it in one of the first two boxes. If I'd end up having to replace it if I give it away now, put it in 'Store.'"

"Most of it will be thrown away, I hope." Our resident storm cloud reappeared.

*Thanks for the input, Jared. Now be quiet!*

She shooed us toward her front door. "Get out of here, both of you. Sammi, I have to plan a funeral for all this stuff of mine."

Left standing on the front steps, Jared and I stared at each other dazedly. He has a Pierce Brosnan sort of handsomeness, though he is broader in the shoulders and more muscular. His complexion is duskier, too, as if he's just flown in from a weekend in Cancun. He carries himself in the same confident 007 swagger and self-assured set of his shoulders. Fleetingly I wished we hadn't met under such thorny circumstances. I'd never seen him when he wasn't angry about something or other. Or maybe this was the sum total of his personality—surly.

I don't understand either Jared's anger or Molly's willingness to admit he has every right to be upset with her. There is an unspoken agreement between them to keep me in the dark about that. Even Ethan Carver danced around the outskirts of the subject. This isn't a situation I enjoy. Neither, apparently, is it one I'm willing to abandon.

I shifted awkwardly from one foot to the other. "I'd better go."

He cleared his throat. "Molly's probably right, you know. You deserve a nice lunch after what you did in there this morning. Frankly, I've never seen her place so picked up—or her so happy about it."

As I watched, he seemed to readjust his mood and attitude to something more appealing. "Do you like seafood, Ms. Smith? I know just the spot."

* * *

The cozy, out-of-the-way place couldn't have been more perfect. Far from lobster traps and deep-sea fishing here in Minnesota, the Gourmet Angler managed to make me think I was eating lobster rolls and fried clams on a bridge overlooking Kennebunkport, Maine. Even the fishing net and splintered oars on the walls seemed just right.

"Nice. I like it."

"Good. Try the sampler platter," Jared suggested. "You can't go wrong."

The good food almost made up for the not-so-good company. Jared was a million miles away. He burst out of his reverie every few minutes to ask me if I had enough cocktail sauce or if I liked the clams and then he would sink back into some deep dark pit of his own making. After one long silence, I cleared my throat and rapped on the table with my spoon to remind him of my presence.

"Wha—" He shoved himself a little straighter in his chair and shook himself as if to clear away the cobwebs.

Hard as I tried to study and comprehend his expression, I couldn't get a handle on it. I'm usually adept at reading people. Perhaps I knew a little too much about Jared to be objective. Or, more accurately, I knew too much about his relationship with his sister.

I've become truly fond of Molly in the short time I've known her. She's bubbly, bright and, much like my friend Wendy, a delight to be around if one can stand the jungle of disarray she tends to create in her vicinity.

"Sorry. I have some pressing things on my mind right now."

"Oh?" I leaned forward slightly.

"I've taken over Molly's files, and it involves some extra work, that's all."

"I'm sure you're missing Molly's presence at Hamilton and

Hamilton. As soon as we sift through her home, we'll be able to apply the same strategies to her office."

The words I'd meant to be consoling seemed only to put him into a deeper funk. He sunk lower in his seat and I felt as though I'd just poked a stick at a sleeping grizzly.

"Did I say something wrong? I'm sorry if I was out of line." I felt a blush redden my cheeks.

"You didn't. You said a perfectly logical thing." He leaned forward and, as if for something to do with his hands, grabbed the small pitcher of cream and dumped it into his coffee. "Unfortunately, I'm not sure if Molly is the cure or the problem." Then he stared into his cup as if surprised to see the milky whiteness of his coffee.

After he'd called the waiter and ordered new coffee—he apparently doesn't even use cream in his coffee—he pulled himself to attention and looked directly into my eyes. "I'm sorry I'm so preoccupied today. You didn't meet me in my best hour. Sometimes I can actually be rather pleasant to be around."

For a millisecond I saw some of Molly's inherent charm in him. "Is there anything I can do? I'm a good listener."

That offer of help shocked him to his senses, and he plucked himself out of the doldrums. I'd edged a little too close to his emotions, and he pulled back with a swiftness that surprised me.

"No, no, not at all. Can I interest you in dessert? The peach crisp is good."

I put my elbows on the table and crossed my arms. Leaning forward, I willed him to look at me. "We'd better talk, Mr. Hamilton…Jared. I don't know what's going on between you and your sister or if you want me butting in, but getting Molly to turn around and shape up in a day or two isn't likely to happen. Possible? Yes. Likely? Not really. That means that you and I will be spending some time together, since you insist on being present as Molly works.

"If there's something I need to know or if you are expecting something more of this than is for Molly's benefit, please tell me. I know you are footing the bill, but you hired me for Molly and she's the one I have to be concerned about."

He looked at me as if I'd just slapped him. "Hidden agendas, you mean? Thanks for your vote of confidence. The basic problem is that my sister can't keep her act together. I can ignore that when we aren't working in the same office. However, since we are, she has to learn how things work at Hamilton and Hamilton and follow protocol, that's all there is to it.

"If Molly were anyone but my sister she'd be have been dismissed already—with no chance of a good recommendation from me." The hardness in his voice surprised me.

Absently he lined up the items at the center of the table— bud vase of flowers, sugar and artificial sweetener holder and ashtray—in a straight line. Then he made sure the used utensils poised on the edge of his plate were straight and refolded the napkin he'd had in his lap.

An avid perfectionist. I know the type. I probably *am* the type in certain circumstances. I could see now that Molly and I were in for it.

On Tuesday morning, I impulsively invited Molly to attend "God's Reflection," a group I've organized at my church. The concept is based on Genesis 1:26:

> *Then God said, 'Let us make humankind in our image, according to our likeness…'"*

And Genesis 9:6:

> *"For in his own image God made humankind."*

Those words stir something very elemental and powerful in me. Imagine *me* created in His likeness as a reflection of His glory, His representative on earth. How awesome.

And humbling.

Thursday afternoon my phone rang. "Samantha Smith speaking?"

"Jared Hamilton here." When I can't see the scowl on his face, his voice is a symphony. "I understand that you've invited my sister to attend a class you're having tonight. I'd like to know more about it."

He was micromanaging again, but Molly had given me full permission to discuss her case with him. Molly, even in this time of seeming trouble, took everything lightly. How those two had been birthed and raised by the same parents is beyond me. It's like a hummingbird and a grizzly bear being blood sister and brother.

"It's a support group for those who want to live up to their potential and desire to reflect God more fully in their lives. I started the group for several of my clients who realized that the disorder in their lives isn't the reflection of God they want to represent to the world. Then clients who don't want to 'fall off the clutter wagon' joined us. Now it's evolved and I've begun to give classes on organizing one's environment. For some, the classes are important. For others it's simply a time for fellowship, encouragement and support."

"Disorganized Anonymous?" There was incredulity in his voice.

"Something like that. I think of it as a way station for the terminally cluttered. Maybe you and Molly should come together."

I'd said it facetiously, of course.

That is why I was so amazed when they walked into the meeting room together later that night.

# Chapter Ten

Ｔrue to their disparate personalities, Molly aimed for a front-row seat but Jared grabbed her elbow and steered her into the last row of chairs and sat there brooding like a dark storm cloud.

"Who's that?" Margaret Wheaton, our pastor's wife, whispered. "I should greet them."

"Go ahead and try but don't get bitten," I muttered to myself, but Margaret heard me.

"What's the problem?"

"No 'problem,' really. It's just a situation I can't figure out." When Molly and Jared were in the same room he was like a caged lion, pacing miserably and obviously trying—and failing—to control his impatience and discontent. Yet he kept coming back for more.

He certainly could have scampered off by now and left Molly and me unchaperoned. I'd begun to sense that he wanted this for Molly almost more than Molly wanted it for herself. It was as if he had more at stake in the organizing of Molly's life than she. Odd—and very puzzling.

Determined to talk with them after class, I began to think

about the icebreaker I would use tonight to begin the class. The toilet paper vs. Kleenex tissue question, I decided. I asked everyone to 'fess up to what was in their purses and pockets. If anyone admitted they were using toilet paper because they hadn't put tissue on the grocery list *again,* it would be a perfect segue into my plan-your-menus-and-make-grocery-lists-in-advance speech. I'm on a personal mission to stamp out all toilet paper used for public blowing. Professional organizers have pet peeves, too, you know.

"I had no idea how remiss I've been in the menu-planning department," Jared said dryly as we left the church together. He'd dozed off a time or two during the evening and not surprisingly had hesitated to join in to the spirited easy-to-cook meal discussion that erupted. For the life of me, I couldn't figure out why he was even there. In fact, he was beginning to make me angry. He looked like an octopus in a pool of goldfish, sitting there, trying to make himself inconspicuous while the ladies in the class feasted their eyes on the only male they'd ever seen cross the threshold of this gathering.

"That was fun!" Molly chortled. "I took notes." Her hands were full of old church bulletins. She'd taken her notes on the white spaces of the programs, making for an interesting written design snaking around the paper.

Mental note: Have Molly start carrying a notebook.

"I'd like to come again if you don't mind, Sammi." Molly's tone was serious.

Jared looked at her sharply.

"I know it sounds crazy—especially to you, Jared—but keeping order is very difficult for me. It feels good to hear what others with my problem do to keep from getting themselves into trouble…er…making messes. It's a relief, in a way, actually, to know I'm not an idiot or the only disorganized person on the planet. I try. I really do. It just never *looks* like it."

"Don't worry," I assured her. "I couldn't run my business or make a living if you were all alone in this. And you are *not* an idiot."

"Good to know." Molly impulsively threw her arms around me and gave me a hug. "Gotta go, you two. I promised my friends Linda and Melody I'd meet them after the meeting. They're picking me up." Within seconds a car pulled into the lot and Molly jumped in. She waved out the window as the car sped away.

That left Jared and me standing in the parking lot, half staring, half glaring at one another. Despite my sense that Jared rode roughshod over Molly's life, I felt a strange reluctance to simply get into my car and drive away. Oddly, although minutes ago he'd seemed desperate to escape, it now seemed that he felt the same disinclination.

"Coffee?" he finally ventured.

I couldn't remember a time when I'd wanted coffee more. Every fiber of my being was yearning for a cup of hot java— at least that's to what I attributed the strange sensation I was feeling—the thought of strong, hot coffee just drawing me in.

Jared could be, I discovered over a turtle mocha, quite charming. As long as his sister's name did not come up, that is.

Every time the conversation edged near Molly or clutter or anything to do with either subject, Jared's eyes turned dark and brooding and I felt him drift away. More than once I snatched him back from the jaws of his own personal pit and discovered that as long as we didn't get near the topic of Molly we could have a surprisingly pleasant discussion.

It was a warm and windless night. As we left the coffee shop I inhaled deeply, breathing in the aroma of freshly cut grass. The moon was brilliant and voluptuous in the inky sky.

"Want to walk?"

"Now? Us?"

He glanced around. "I don't see anyone else. It's too nice an evening to waste inside, don't you think?" He nodded toward the winking glints of moonlight reflecting off the nearby lake.

"I love the nighttime," I commented as we strolled.

"Not everyone does," he commented.

"It's like God wraps us in a soft, dark velvet cushion and keeps us safe when we're most vulnerable. When I was a little girl, I used to think the moon was God's peek hole down to us and every time a cloud went by and blocked the moon, it was Him blinking."

"What about the nights you couldn't see the moon?"

"I just assumed He was peeking down at someone else far away. I didn't have much comprehension of the rotation of the earth back then."

"It's a nice thought." He was silent for a long time before he said, "I never liked the dark much. I thought it was boring. I had to go to bed. My mother told me that if I'd had my own way, I would have slept only at the darkest part of the night and awakened with the sun.

"Molly," he continued, "always thought she was missing something if I was up and she was still sleeping. Of course, she was so high maintenance even then that I was never quite sure if I was glad she was up to follow me around or wished she'd sleep until noon."

"She loves you a great deal," I ventured.

"And I love her." The statement sounded like a burden. "But, Ms. Smith, I'm not going to let that get in the way of what needs to be done."

*So much for warm and fuzzy brother/sister relationships.*
Every time I thought I might be able to like Jared Ham-

ilton, he pulled another rug out from under me. I put another black check mark against him in the tally I'd begun keeping in my head.

## Chapter Eleven

Molly called my office on Monday, giggling.

"What's so funny?" She certainly is sunny, considering all that's going on in her life.

"I eavesdropped on Jared and his friend Ethan last night. They were talking about *you*."

*Oh, puleese! Spare me!*

"I don't want to hear this."

"It's all good…well, fairly good, anyway…and I thought you'd want to know." Supposing that she was correct in that assumption, she dived into her story.

"Ethan asked Jared how he likes you."

"Molly, don't go there."

"No, this is good. Really! Jared dodged the question by telling him that *I* liked you and that's enough. Of course, that's not what Ethan wanted to know. He feels responsible for the two of you meeting. He's taking an interest in your relationship."

Terrific. Just what Jared and I need when we're butting heads—onlookers.

"Jared thinks you don't like him and that you are suspicious of his motives with me." Molly laughed. "Can you believe it?"

It wasn't exactly a newsflash.

"He says you don't trust him because he's threatened to fire me."

*Well, duh!*

"And Ethan nailed my brother to the wall with that one. He told Jared that he just doesn't like the idea of you thinking of him being the 'bad guy' in my life."

All this was giving me a big headache. I was hired by these people to get them organized, not be one of the stars in their ongoing soap opera.

"I think Ethan's right," Molly continued. "My brother isn't accustomed to being out of favor with a beautiful woman."

*A beautiful woman? Me?*

"Molly, I don't need to know this." I felt as though I was in junior high again, playing that obnoxious "He said, she said" game.

"Jared tried to deny it, but Ethan told him that if he couldn't see it, he should get himself a white cane and a seeing-eye dog. 'She's incredible,' Ethan told him, 'that blond hair like spun sugar and those eyes! Big, blue, mesmeric…she's not just beautiful, Jared, she's *riveting.*'" Molly giggled. "Isn't that fabulous?"

"Sounds like I should start batting my eyelashes at Ethan," I joked, not wanting to let her know she'd really flummoxed me with this. I am not in the habit of thinking of my looks at all—and never as beautiful. Nordic, yes. Beautiful, no.

"Jared said the same thing, but Ethan wouldn't give in. He told my brother that he is accustomed to women flirting with him. And because you don't fall at his feet, Jared's ego is bothering him. I think it really stunned Jared to hear that."

It certainly stunned me. My cheeks felt as though they were on fire. This was too much information.

Molly didn't seem to hear me. She was having too much fun developing this fantasy of hers. "Then Ethan and Jared went to play racquetball."

"What a relief," I muttered.

"And Ethan told me later that Jared *slaughtered* him."

"What are friends for?"

"I know what's going on when Jared does that. He's frustrated. Ethan came too close to my brother's true emotions talking about you like that."

*Deluded, deluded, deluded. This girl is completely deluded.*

Molly added sagely, "Just wait. You'll see."

I didn't say it aloud, but I decided then and there that I was *not* hanging around to find out.

# Chapter Twelve

If men were shoes, Jared Hamilton would be waffle-stompers, treading over everybody and everything to get to his personal destination. If women were shoes, Molly would be a pair of soft, fluffy bedroom slippers that keep getting lost. And I would be stilettos just waiting to grind a heel into the top of Jared's hiking boots.

"Why? I don't get this, Molly. You'll have to tell me why."

I had her alone for once. Jared was forced to tend to business in his own office while we painstakingly sorted through the jumble in Molly's. "Your brother is a stalker. He's been after us since the first day we started to work together. Doesn't he trust me?"

I don't have much in the way of ego because I know that only God can take credit for whatever I might do right, but Jared is getting on my nerves, the few I have left. I'm going crazy being observed hour after hour by him as his sister and I try to make headway through Molly's muddle.

The woman is sweet, precious, generous, giving and completely without organizational skills. I don't doubt for a moment that she has the intelligence to learn them, but she just doesn't seem to care.

Neatness is not even a blip on Molly's radar screen of desires. For her it ranks right up there with wanting a root canal or ingrown toenails.

Jared, on the other hand, thinks that a pile of magazines is an eyesore, a stack of papers on a desk an anathema and a disorganized office a deadly sin.

And I thought *I* was exacting!

"Don't be too hard on him, Sammi. He's doing what he thinks is best for me, that's all."

"But you're a grown woman. Why can't *you* do what's best for you?" I sat back to study her and was surprised to see tears in her eyes. "Molly?"

"Jared's right. I'm incompetent."

Unbidden anger flared in me. "He told you that?"

"No, but he thinks it. So whatever Jared wants, I'll do." She wiped away the tears with the back of her hand. "Anything."

Jared Hamilton had his poor sister hopping and dancing to his wishes like she was a marionette and he, a puppeteer.

"Have you considered that Jared may have some issues of his own?" I ventured.

"Jared is a successful man, highly regarded in business," Molly huffed. "He didn't get here without careful planning and hard work. He has to be meticulous and exacting in order to be where he is."

"Why do you defend him?" I asked gently.

"Because you can never imagine what he's put up with from me. Never. I love him. He's the best brother in the world." And that was the end of that subject. Molly was willing to turn herself inside out to make her demanding brother happy.

Because I'm the hired help, it doesn't matter that I can't see the reason why.

\* \* \*

I groaned when the doorbell rang. Just out of the shower, I'd decided to test the self-adhering curlers that Wendy gave me. They were the size of soup cans and, Wendy said, perfect for creating a smooth, sophisticated hairdo. She'd also given me a facial mask, cucumber and seaweed, I think, or maybe it's grass clippings and zucchini. I'd put foam separators between my toes so my pedicure could dry, whitening strips on my teeth and my softest, coziest and least flattering red-and-gray sweats. I glanced in the mirror. With all the bright colors and distorted features, I looked like some little kid's worst nightmare, worse, even, than a clown doll, the kind that lurks in children's closets and gives them scary dreams.

I shuffled toward the door, keeping my toes wide spread and my neck stiff so as not to upset the precarious pyramid of rollers. Not only was my face beginning to harden, my teeth squeaked and the facial mask was beginning to smell very earthy. Not flower petals and fresh breezes earthy, either. More like barnyard-and-compost-heap earthy. Wendy must have bought all this stuff on sale.

"Who is it?" I inquired at the door, but my mouth wasn't moving well because of the rock-hard mask. I was also paralyzed by my reluctance to take off the whitening strip until my thirty minutes were up. My words came out more like a breathy "whoiszit?"

I peered through the peek hole but all I could see was a sweatshirt-clad shoulder with a bit of the Timberwolves logo on it. It had to be Ben, the all-time, number-one Timberwolves fan. I reached to open the door. Ben wouldn't notice if I dressed myself in garbage bags secured with duct tape.

"Hullocominimmm...." My mumbled greeting ended sharply. "Jrd?"

"Sammi? Is that you?"

Jared Hamilton peered into the two peek holes in my facial mask that I'd left for my eyes. His nose wrinkled as he got a whiff of the facial's "earthy scent."

I whipped off the whitening strips and opened my mouth wide, cracking the concretelike facial into bits. "What are you doing here?"

He bent over to pick up a few of the shards of green facial mask that fell to the floor. "Your face is breaking. Do you want me to pick it up?"

I spun to run to the bathroom to chisel off the rest of the mask but forgot that my toes were swathed in foam rubber. The rubber stuck to the hardwood floor, pitching me over the back of a white canvas-covered chair and face first into the seat cushion. I teetered, feet in the air, for a moment before righting myself. As I did so, I saw the imprint of a minty green face on the seat of the chair—my own sort of death mask imposed right onto the cushion of the newest piece of furniture in the house. The term death mask is appropriate. I was dying from a case of terminal embarrassment. Mortified by my lack of dignity and even my lack of balance, I staggered to my feet in a vain effort to recover my poise.

That, of course, didn't happen. My curlers abandoned ship, sprang loose and pulled from my hair. I could feel them dangling around my shoulders like decorations on a Christmas tree. Then, one by one, they tumbled out of my hair and onto the floor.

The horrified expression on Jared's face said it all. All there was to say, at least, until he started laughing. And laughing. And laughing.

I scuttled, crablike, toward the bathroom and didn't come out until I'd found my normal skin color, my hair and my pearly white teeth. Then I returned to the living room where Jared was on his hands and knees with a bucket, a rag and cleanser carefully removing my visage from the seat cushion.

He looked up, half worried and half laughing. "Are you all right?"

"Yes. Thank you for asking," I answered with as much dignity as I could muster.

"This is going to come out, but it will take a little work. I didn't want to spread the stain, but if you just blot it like this…"

"Thank you. I can do it. Cleaning is one of my specialties, you know."

*How am I ever going to live this down?*

He unfolded himself and stood up, eyeing me cautiously, as if he didn't know what to expect to happen next. He had the right to be nervous. *I* certainly was.

"I see I caught you at a bad time—during your beauty ritual." He said "beauty ritual" as though referring to the horrific and mysterious procedure the Egyptians used to embalm mummies.

"My friend Wendy gave me some new products to try and…"

"You don't have to explain. I grew up with Molly, remember? I'd challenge any woman to come up with something my sister hasn't already sprung on me, Sammi. No need to be embarrassed."

He'd managed to say exactly the right thing to make me feel better. I looked up at him with a thankful smile and saw his expression had turned into one of complete, unadulterated horror.

Jared stared over my shoulder toward my bedroom door. He lifted one hand and pointed to the opening.

"What on earth is *that*?"

I turned to see Zelda yawning and stretching in the doorway, her skinned and skinny body writhing in bliss, her gigantic ears quivering with pleasure. To the uninitiated in the world of hairless cats, it must have been a sight to behold.

"That's my cat, Zelda. She's a sphynx. We're playing spa night. I just gave her a bath and cleaned her ears with oil. She's feeling frisky."

Wrinkled skin is highly desirable in the sphynx breed and Zelda is show-cat perfect. Her little muzzle is exceptionally wrinkled, as is the skin between and around her shoulders. Her head is longer than it is wide, her skull rounded but with a flat forehead and prominent cheekbones. Of course, if one didn't know the breed, that might seem a little creepy. She also has very large ears, startling, wide-set lemon-shaped eyes and a whip of a tail. Her hind legs are slightly longer than her front so she always looks like she's walking downhill. What's more, a sphynx's paw pads are very thick and their toes long and slender so Zelda appears to be walking on air cushions. A large female, Zelda is almost ten pounds of luxurious, exotic, alien-looking feline.

Jared gawked at her, dumbstruck. Zelda stared back at Jared with disdain. He had no distinguishing features whatsoever to make him interesting to her, no catnip mouse on his lapel, not even a large, semitransparent set of ears. She turned to give him a full view of her bony behind, flicked her tail and, ignoring us both, sat down to bathe herself.

"Is it supposed to look like that? What happened to its hair?"

"Shhhh." I put a finger to my lips. "Don't say anything to hurt her feelings. Besides, I don't think she sees any blue ribbons on you, either."

He glanced around the room as if looking for someone or something sane or normal. Finding no one, his gaze came back to me.

"Is that really a cat?" His brows furrowed. He looked particularly handsome when he was perplexed.

"What else could it be?" Hopping on one foot and then the other, I pulled the sponges from between my toes.

"A cross between a fruit bat and a Chihuahua? A chemistry experiment gone wrong? Doctor Frankenstein's dirty little secret?"

"Would you like to pet her?"

He recoiled slightly. "What does it feel like?"

"*She* feels like the chamois you use to wash your car, only she's nice and warm." I moved toward Zelda and bent to pick her up. She immediately began to purr and knead her paws into my arm.

Jared put out a tentative hand to touch her and drew back quickly. "She feels like a suede jacket that's been lying in the sun."

"Good analogy." I scratched Zelda behind the ears. "Hear that, sweetie?"

Zelda yawned so widely that I believed that had Jared looked, he could have seen the inside of the tip of her tail.

At that moment, Imelda came trotting out of my room with the decimated Manolo Blahnik in her mouth. She went right to Jared, put her paws on his chest as if to show him the doggie pedicure I'd just given her, hot pink and purple nails, faux rhinestones and all.

"What kind of a zoo do you have here, anyway?"

"Yours truly included?" I asked sweetly, knowing that at the moment I was looking every bit as weird as my beloved pets.

"No, I didn't mean…I…" Jared looked to me for help.

I thrust Zelda into his arms. "I'll be back in a minute. I have to brush my teeth. I think I have chips of that facial in my mouth."

It was actually closer to five minutes by the time I'd rinsed my mouth and pulled on a pair of jeans and a sweatshirt. When I returned to the living room both Zelda and Imelda were on Jared's lap.

"You got their *Good Housekeeping* seal of approval, I see. That's not easy. Good going." I dropped into the chair across from him.

"Thanks. I think." He looked at me, puzzled. "Somehow I never thought of you…like this."

I glanced around the room as if seeing it for the first time. Sleek, Danish modern furniture, maple floors, bright, modern art posters, sculptures Wendy had made in some of her funkier phases and baskets everywhere to corral clutter and keep it out of site. And Zelda and Imelda, of course, both living, breathing forms of contemporary art.

"What does 'like this' mean?" I asked.

"Untraditional? Arty? A little crazy?"

"That's me in a nutshell," I agreed amiably. "Now, what are you doing here?"

# *Chapter Thirteen*

When I'd opened my front door to see Jared standing there my first instinct had been to run and hide under the bed with Imelda. Then I remembered that he knew nothing of Molly's informational report of the conversation he'd had with Ethan. *Whew.*

Jared shifted uncomfortably, as if he, too, was wondering why he was here.

Maybe I'd made him curious and he wanted to see if I practiced what I preached.

That's the theory Wendy had come to and vocalized over dinner last night.

"You're a curiosity to him, Sammi. Look at the man. He's incredible-looking, smart, wealthy, has great clothes and a sports car. He's not accustomed to women not being interested in him. He's not used to women playing hard to get."

"I'm not *playing* 'hard to get'!" I'd said. "I don't want to get got!"

"Whatever *that* means," Wendy had said, grinning.

But it is true. I'm not *playing* hard to get. It's no act. Every vibe I give off should tell him that this is no game. Why Jared and I seem to be the only people who don't look at each other as a romantic opportunity in the making, I don't know.

"He doesn't realize that getting close to you now is going to be like climbing Mount Everest in tennis shoes and jogging shorts," Wendy had observed. "He simply isn't prepared for you."

*Well, I'm not prepared for him, either.*

I wish everyone would quit playing matchmaker and philosopher and let me live my life without their offerings of pop psychology. For one thing, if Molly hadn't told me about Jared's conversation with Ethan, I'd be a whole lot more relaxed right now.

"I was in the neighborhood and I thought I'd drop by and deliver this." He pulled a Bently fountain pen from his pocket. "Is it yours?"

A wash of relief spread over me. This visit had nothing to do with me at all, other than the fact that I owned and had lost a very expensive pen. "You found it! Did I drop it at Molly's?" I reached out for pen gratefully. "Thank you. It was a gift from my friend, Ben. Every once in a while he surreptitiously checks to see if I'm still using it. I didn't look forward to telling him I'd lost it."

Jared raised an eyebrow but said nothing. The pen was an expensive one—upwards of two hundred and fifty dollars, and no doubt he was wondering what kind of relationship I had with a man who would give me such costly gifts.

The truth be known, the pen said very little about my relationship with Ben. He'd purchased the pen because he thought it was funny—Ben and *Bent*ly. He's always chosen to purchase his clothes at Goodwill and lavish gifts on his friends and family instead.

My good manners finally welled to the surface. I gestured him toward the kitchen. "As long as you're here—and have already cleaned my furniture—would you like a cup of chai or coffee?"

"Coffee is fine."

Jared sat at my small stainless steel-topped table and took in the room while I brewed the coffee. My kitchen has a Nordic feel with its simple maple cabinets and blue and white color scheme. There are the painted red Dala horses I love, beautiful blown glass bowls and a family of trolls decorating the tops of my cupboards, but I prefer to have nothing on my counter but the coffeepot and a cluster of yellow and red tulips in a bright blue glass vase. I like things simple, tidy and spotless. Wendy says that the man I should be dating is Mr. Clean.

I set the coffee cup in front of him with a plate of cream-filled pirouettes and butter cookies. He looked like a bull in a china shop looming over the delicate things so I went to the freezer, pulled out another container and extracted four chocolate chip oatmeal cookies the size of salad plates, put them in the microwave and defrosted them.

When I brought those to the table, Jared gave a sigh of relief.

"Sorry about the girlie stuff. I forget men like cookies bigger than their little finger."

"You have a lovely home," he said politely.

"Thanks. I've lived here over a year now."

"Just moved to the cities?"

"Oh, no. I grew up here." I folded into a chair and looked at him with palpable curiosity. "And you?"

"Me, too. Kenwood area."

"Not too shabby."

"I suppose not."

The conversation ground to a halt. Jared seemed almost relieved to have Zelda jump into his lap, put her overlarge foot pads on the front of his coat and jam her nose under his chin. For a moment, he didn't know what to do with his hands.

"She likes you!" For some reason it pleased me inordinately. "She usually doesn't warm up to people so quickly."

Jared stroked her back.

She's soft and warm to the touch and when she arched into his hand, I knew Jared could feel her boney spine beneath his fingers. Despite her weirdness, there is something endearing about Zelda. She is blissfully unaware of anything but the force of her personality and she was turning it all on Jared. He scratched her and she purred. He gathered her to his chest and she snuggled in. He talked softly into her ear and she kneaded his arm approvingly with her claws. He slipped off his watch to keep it from catching on her skin. She tipped her head and her rhinestone collar flashed in the light.

Zelda was doing her magic act and Jared fell under her spell.

"So how do you feel about my naked cat now?" I watched them as I sipped my coffee.

"Not what I expected."

"Things seldom are."

"She's amazing." He looked down at Zelda, who was batting with one paw at the tip of his shirt collar.

"The breed is very intelligent and friendly. Zelda is always ready to cuddle or to play. In fact—" and I reddened a little "—she likes to sleep under the covers with me."

Fortunately, before Jared had time to think about that, Imelda pranced into the kitchen looking, as many labradoodles do, like an oversize, curly-haired toy, carrying her favorite high heel like a bone between her teeth, her bright purple-and-pink toenails clicking on the hardwood floor.

After he left, I began to wonder how Jared really saw me—a green face print on the seat of my chair, my wiry fur-challenged cat and goofy flop-eared dog who Jared insisted on calling a retrievapoo instead of a labradoodle. When Imelda wasn't chewing on a high heel, she was sitting on it, protecting it from who-knows-what—other dogs with shoe fetishes, perhaps. I'm sure none of it fits with the brisk, no-nonsense woman he thought he'd hired to help his sister.

And why that even mattered to me made no sense at all.

# Chapter Fourteen

"Anybody home?" I pushed Molly's door open and walked inside. Today was the day we'd planned to organize what Molly calls the "inner sanctum"—her bedroom. Molly's home reminds me of a delta, layer upon layer of sediment, stuff washed up upon more stuff until it becomes a new landmass all its own. It's no wonder Molly is overwhelmed and has given up trying to sort through this.

We'd cleared the floor in one small spot on the carpet yesterday and I'd left her with the assignment to keep excavating. I know it was slow going with Molly squealing every few minutes over a sweater she thought she'd lost or a missing earring revealed. It was like being on an archeological dig—slow, tedious and with the tantalizing promise of intriguing discoveries at the end. In this case, the discovery was Molly's bedroom floor.

I suppose I should thank her for toughening her brother up for me.

I recalled last night when Jared had shown up at my front door bearing my lost pen, and cringed. Why he hadn't run off screaming, I still haven't figured out. I'd looked as bizarre as

Zelda. I never say Zelda is bizarre in her presence, but she *is* pretty peculiar when compared to others of her species. I'd smelled like compost, looked like death warmed over—except for my sparkling white teeth—and been as clumsy as all three Stooges. If I *had* wanted to impress him, it was all over now.

Once I'd gotten over the shock of seeing him at my front door I'd realized that we do have something in common. He'd known exactly what to do to get my face print off the seat cushion, he'd put his own cup and saucer in the sink when he was finished with his coffee and he'd even plumped the pillow he'd rested against as we visited on the couch.

If he weren't so determined to fire his own sister and make her life miserable, I might actually have considered seeing him socially. Oh, well. There have to be more tidy fish in the sea.

"Molly? Are you here?" Odd. She always welcomes me the moment I knock. In fact, Molly is always happy to see me. She believes I'm her lifeline, a way out of the messes of her own making.

I heard a small noise in the bedroom and followed the sound.

"Molly?" I peered through the doorway to see her curled into a ball on her chair, feet tucked under her. Tears ran down her cheeks and when she looked up at me, there was desperation in her eyes.

"Sammi, what's wrong with me?" was her greeting.

"Nothing is 'wrong' with you other than you're crying. What's happened?" I hurried across the floor to her. Still in her pajamas and slippers, she looked like a pink, fuzzy little girl curled there on the chair with a soulful, heartbroken expression on her face. Sometimes Molly seemed so vulnerable it was difficult to remember she was not still a teenager.

"Nothing! Can't you tell?" She gestured toward the room, which looked exactly the same as it had when I'd left the day before. "I didn't get a thing done. I started, but then I found some mail and went to the kitchen to get a knife to open it. That reminded me that I hadn't eaten dinner so I fixed myself something to eat as I read the mail. Of course there were bills so I had to get my checkbook out to pay them. In my checkbook I found the phone number of an old friend I'd been meaning to call. Next thing I know we'd talked two hours and it was midnight and I was exhausted. My brother is right. I am hopeless!"

"Did he say that?" I felt a surge of anger within me.

"He didn't say it. *I* did. And it's true. I've spent my whole life muddling things up and he's had to bail me out. I can't even get this done properly! I'm like a hummingbird that flits from one flower to another. I can't stay in one place long enough to make any headway whatsoever."

She looked at me with bleary eyes. "I know you aren't happy with Jared because he's grown tired of the messes I create, but it's not his fault. It's mine!"

"I'm not exactly unhappy with Jared," I began tentatively.

"Yes, you are. I can see it in your eyes. You don't even *like* my brother, do you?"

Her question hit me like a slap. For someone who considers herself nonjudgmental, I'd certainly fallen into the trap. Jared is a conundrum for me. I'd seen him angry and cordial, loving and hard-nosed, determined and gentle, and still I was clueless as to who he was as a man. And, no, I didn't like him, if for no other reason than for the way he treated Molly.

"Go take a shower. You'll feel better. Then we can make some headway in here."

But Molly, for once, was suddenly difficult to distract.

"You really don't like him."

"It doesn't matter what I think…."

"It matters to me. I'd do anything in the world for Jared. He's the best brother a woman could have."

"Even if he fires you?"

Molly winced and was quiet. She couldn't find a way to argue with that.


By evening, we had made remarkable progress. Her closets looked like *Better Homes & Gardens* material, there was a place for everything and everything was in its place.

We sat on the floor in her bedroom and admired our work.

"It's perfect," she said breathily. "I'm going to visit here every day."

"Visit?"

"If I move to a hotel, I wouldn't be here to undo our work. What do you think of that?"

I stared at her for a moment before I realized she was teasing. I put my hand to my heart and sighed. "You scared me. For a minute I thought you were *serious!*"

"I'm like Pigpen in the *Peanuts* comic," she said ruefully. "There's a little cloud of clutter floating around me all the time, wherever I go."

I decided to ask the question that's been burning in me. "Molly, do you ever think that your brother might be unfair about you? Do you think he's too harsh, threatening to fire you?"

Molly chewed on her upper lip. "You don't know the whole story, Sammi. All I can say is whatever Jared does, I deserve. He's a great guy. If you'd met him without me in the picture, I think you two would have hit it off."

She sighed. "Here I am messing things up for Jared again. Maybe, just maybe, under different circumstances, you could be my sister-in-law instead of my mentor. What would you think of that?"

"Sister-in-law?" I was speechless. So that was the direction Molly's mind was turning in. Suddenly I was in a very big hurry to be done with this job and out of Jared Hamilton's life.

* * *

"You can quit slamming pots and pans around, you know. He's not here to bug you." Wendy sat at the table knitting while Zelda and Imelda unrolled her ball of yarn and tangled it around chair legs as they played.

"I'm making dinner. This has nothing to do with Jared. I can't believe you said that!" I punctuated the sentence with an extra clank of a pan.

Wendy narrowed her eyes and stared at me. "Methinks the lady doth protest too much."

"What does Shakespeare have to do with anything?"

"I've heard a dozen times tonight that you think this Jared Hamilton is a jerk…or a cad…or a creep. He must have some redeeming qualities. What about those?"

"Flushed down the toilet, that's what. Molly Hamilton brings out something protective and nurturing in me. Weirdly, I feel driven to protect her from her own brother."

"So, then," Wendy said, wisely changing the subject. "Have you seen Ben lately?"

"He was over last night. He wanted to hook my TiVo to my alarm clock so that I could wake up to *The Brady Bunch*."

"The man is a genius and a wreck waiting to happen." Wendy knitted and purled awhile before she spoke again. "Have you noticed that even though you are the most organized person in the world, you attract messies like me and Ben…and Molly?"

I hadn't really thought of it, but what she said is true. I love tidiness—and people who aren't.

"Maybe I have a missionary complex," I offered. "I want to save you from yourselves."

"Hah!" Wendy jabbed the knitting needles into the scarf and dropped it to the floor. Zelda and Imelda pounced and I knew that in a few minutes they'd undo all the work she had done. I bit my lip and stayed silent. It was Wendy's scarf. If she wanted it to look like the snarled underside of a tapestry weaving, so be it.

"This job has got your dander up," Wendy said bluntly. "And I think it's Jared Hamilton who's really got you going."

"Not *me*. Look what a state he's got his sister in."

"It's not your business."

Wendy was right, but somehow I'd made it my business anyway and I wasn't happy about it.

That night I dreamed that I was rubbing my hand over Jared Hamilton's strong, masculine, stubbled jaw and he was loving my touch. He even hummed softly in my ear, a contented sound…a purr. Then I woke up and realized I'd been stroking Zelda, who'd burrowed into my arms and allowed me to hold her in a warm embrace.

# *Chapter Fifteen*

We are nearing the finish line and not a moment too soon.

My affection for Molly is growing in an inverse relation-ship to my dislike for her brother. He set up camp at her house again when we moved to Molly's home office, and demanded to see every scrap of paper or envelope we ran across.

"Molly, I can't believe the unmitigated, unimaginable mess you've got here! How you cope is beyond me." He threw the papers he'd been looking at onto the floor and ran his fingers through his hair in frustration, a gesture I'd become far too familiar with lately. "What am I going to do with you?"

Molly froze for a moment to stare at him. "What *are* you going to do with me, Jared? I need to know."

The sparks between them flew so hot and bright that I found myself backing away. This was a mostly invisible conversation, the kind only siblings or mates can have with one another.

Then Jared remembered that I was there, sighed, rose to his feet and walked out the door without saying a word or looking back.

When I turned to Molly, I was surprised to see the expres-sion on her face. She looked concerned. Not for herself but for *me.* "Don't worry about that, Sammi, he's just having a bad day. He'll be fine tomorrow."

"Why do you keep protecting him, Molly? I don't get it. Your job is on the line and all you care about is whether *I* like him or not?"

She looked at me as though I were a very slow child who couldn't comprehend the ramifications of what had just happened. "It's *okay,* Sammi. It really is. You don't have to take on my battle with my brother. Really."

But I had. I'd stepped across a line and I knew it. I'd become Molly's friend, not merely her consultant. It was time for me to quit.

She didn't take the news of my resignation well.

"Are you sure I can do this alone?" Molly fussed unhappily. "Can I call you if I need help?"

"Call me as a friend anytime. If you need professional services, I have the names of some great people you can use. I wrote Jared a note to let him know what I've decided. He'll get back to me when he returns from his business trip so you don't have to tell him, okay?" I put my hand on her arm because she looked as though she was about to burst into tears.

"I don't see why…"

"I've become too close to this situation, Molly. I'm no longer objective about you and your brother. I should have kept my distance and not become so involved with you. It's a policy I have. It wasn't professional." I felt myself tear up. "I'm sorry."

"You mean you can either be a coach or a friend but not both?"

"It's my policy, Molly." I took her hand. "But I am still your friend."

"I know how protective you've been of me, but it's not necessary. Really."

"There you go again, defending Jared."

Molly looked as though there were something she desperately wanted to tell me. She opened her mouth to speak but closed it again.

"I won't go away mad," I said with more lightness than I felt. "I'll just go away."

She leaned to give me a hug. Her smile returned. "I wish you'd met us in different circumstances. Jared and I are really cool people, you know."

"I know." *About you, at least.*

As I drove away from Molly's house, I took a peek in my rearview mirror. She was waving. And the mystery of her obstinate brother was no closer to being cleared up than the day I'd met him in Ethan Carver's office almost a month ago.

"Your mail is here," Ben announced. He's come twice this week to work on my furnace. It scares me a little, but he's promised he isn't hooking it up to anything else in the basement—especially not the water heater, the freezer or propane tank.

"Thanks, sweetie." I gave him a hug. I'm more grateful than ever for Ben these days. He never has a dark moment or a flash of annoyance. I appreciate him more after having spent time with Jared.

"No problem." He held up a large, impressive looking envelope. "What's this? Looks important."

"Probably more expensive junk mail. Here, let me have it." I reached for the piece and noticed Molly's return address in the left-hand corner. "What on earth…"

I tore into the envelope, which looked very much like an oversize wedding invitation. The inside envelope was addressed simply "Sammi." Inside that was a formal-looking gift certificate.

*This certificate entitles you to a weekend stay June 22-24 at The Oasis, Minnesota's finest hotel and spa. Services included in this gift are two massages, one body wrap, manicure, pedicure, and two other services of your choice. This weekend is complements of...*

A note had been added to the printed invitation.

*Sammi, this is for all you've done for me. You've been a port in the storm. Now, if you could only like and understand my brother like I do, everything would be so wonderful. Still, I realize how hard it is for you to see me like this. Just know it's not all Jared's fault.*
    *Have fun at the spa and think of me!*

And there was Molly's signature, scrawled on the bottom line with a little smiley face and a series of exclamation points.

"What is it?" Ben peered curiously over my shoulder. He was holding Imelda, who thinks she is a lap dog, even though she's the size of a full-grown lab or standard poodle. She panted and her hot, doggie breath warmed my neck.

"A certificate for a weekend at a spa."

"Cool. Who from?"

"A former client of mine."

"Wow. She must really like you." Ben moved Imelda so that she draped over his arm and shoulder. She managed to hang there, happily imitating a bad fur boa.

Anytime Imelda is picked up and Zelda is left on the floor, Imelda is pleased. She has issues with Zelda being able to leap her way from floor to chair to kitchen counter to the top of the refrigerator. I don't really blame her since Zelda then sits hissing and taunting poor earthbound Imelda. And that's only one of the antics I see those two perform. I shudder to think what happens when I'm not home and they have the run of the place. I have never quite decided how the two of them managed to empty all my bottom cupboards while I was out on a date. I found tortilla chips in the bathroom, a scrub brush in my closet and an entire bag of navy beans chewed open and spread across my bed.

Neither pet approved of that guy from the get-go. When, on our second date, Zelda snagged his trousers and Imelda ate the wallet that had fallen into the cushions of my couch, I knew that he did not have their stamp of approval. Interestingly enough, Jared, who doesn't have *my* stamp of approval, has received theirs. Maybe their instincts are dulling.

"She shouldn't have done that," I murmured, gazing at the beautiful invitation. It was a wonderful thank-you gift. I can't accept it, of course, but I appreciate the thought.


"But you have to do it!" Molly said the next day when she called. "Don't refuse. You've helped me so much that I'll never be able to repay you. Take this weekend for yourself. Please?"

I glanced at the calendar. The weekend of the 23$^{rd}$ was open.

"It's too much, Molly."

"I have a friend who is a part owner. I never pay full price. Don't argue with me, Sammi. Just go. I'm not taking 'no' for an answer. I don't want any more disappointment this week."

My antennae went up. "'Disappointment'? What do you mean?"

Molly sighed deeply. "If you must know, Jared and I had a little trouble."

"What kind of 'trouble'?" I was suddenly filled with misgiving.

"I made a little mistake and he fired me."

"Fired you? What was the 'little' mis—"

Molly cut me short.

"I don't want to talk about it right now. Right now I want to enjoy giving you this gift. The very best thing you can do for me is accept it and go there to enjoy it. You and I will have plenty of time to discuss the other issue when you get back." Her voice was firm.

"But what about you? Are you okay?"

"I refuse to discuss it," Molly said firmly.

What Molly lacks in organizational skills, she makes up for in persuasive abilities. Almost before I knew what had happened, I'd promised that I would go to the spa the coming weekend. Molly made it sound as if not doing it would have been a slap in her face.

"It's over-the-top, really," I told Wendy later. "She wouldn't have had to…"

"But she did, so accept graciously and enjoy it."

"I suppose you're right."

"Of course I am," Wendy said cheerfully. With the promise painfully extracted from me, she added, "The weekend is only four days away. I'll help you plan what to pack."

*The Oasis Spa Welcomes You!*

I looked at the engraved sign over the door and then back at the taillights of Wendy's car as she drove away.

It had seemed like a good idea at the time, me riding with her to the spa and staying there while Wendy went up north to visit her sister and brother-in-law. But now that she was leaving and my only means of escape was vanishing, I began to feel trapped. What if I hated it here? What if the masseuse was Hildegard the Horrible and she pummeled me into a visit to an emergency room? What if spa food meant a sprig of parsley, a wisp of carrot and a gallon of water? What if…

*Snap out of it! You're awful-izing again.*

Awful-izeing is my term for someone who can't look at a problem without immediately going to the worst possible scenario or outcome. Many of my clients awful-ize. "I'll never get this mess sorted out," or "I'm going to have to live like this forever," or, my favorite, "It's genetic. Everyone in my family does it."

Still, I felt a flutter of excitement in my belly as I looked around the foyer. There was a lavish marble floor beneath my feet, intricate columns and arches leading toward several long halls, a fountain in which a lovely maiden poured endless water from an ewer into a pool and piped-in music that made my muscles relax just listening to it.

By the time I reached my room—a suite decorated with voluptuous cherubs and every hue of pink—I knew that this was the best gift I'd ever received and if I were smart, I'd take advantage of it.

Wendy had picked out my "spa wardrobe" and included two sleek, body hugging leotards and two dresses to wear for the formal evening meals. One was a clever, long-sleeved knit that covered me neck-to-knee in front, and left my back bare. The other dress was sleeveless and the pale icy-blue of my eyes. In it I look like a Valkyrie, one of those maidens from Norse myth, Amazons with "golden hair and snowy arms." I could practically hear music from Wagner's libretto *Die Walküre* playing in my mind. Brunhilde-on-the-move, that's me.

There was a tiny knock on the door as I hung my clothing in the closet.

"Come in!"

A willowy, reed-thin woman entered and glided toward me as if she were on wheels. Her hair was pulled so tightly away from her face that her eyes slanted much like Zelda's, sort of a ponytail-cum-facelift. Her skin gleamed—a result, no doubt, of some of the spa treatments offered here. The list was so long that I'd given up deciding which procedures I should choose.

"I am Olga, manager of the spa." She drew out her name so it sounded like Ooolgaaaa. She thrust a list into my hand. "Ms. Molly Hamilton has chosen these treatments as part of your spa package. Are they acceptable to you?"

Molly had thought of everything—including the treatments my invitation had called "optional." I barely glanced at the list. "Whatever Molly thinks is fine with me." Frankly, after viewing the spa menu, I didn't care. It all sounded wonderful.

"Good." Ooolgaaaa referred to her wristwatch. "You are scheduled for a light lunch at one, after which you report to the spa area. They also have your schedule there and will move you from treatment room to treatment room. Please bring your bathing suit as you will have time to sit in our whirlpool during the afternoon." She pointed to a fluffy pink robe hanging in the closet and then to a pair of matching slides. "Please wear these. And have a wonderful stay." Her "wonderful" sounded like voooderfuuul, but I got the drift.

"Right. Lunch first." I checked the schedule she'd given me. "Table twenty-eight in the green dining room. Then the spa rooms."

She gave me an approving smile, as if I'd passed some undisclosed test. "Good. Please do not be late for or miss any of your appointments. We are tightly booked this weekend." And she rolled out of my room on those ball-bearing feet of hers.

I looked down at my legs. Trying to get into the part of vacationer, I'd worn white caprilike pants and a splashy multi-colored tunic. It was a little loud, but Wendy had tie-dyed it for me and I wanted to wear it somewhere.

Feeling more festive than I had in weeks, I headed toward the first meal of the rest of my weekend.

## Chapter Sixteen

The dining room of the Oasis is as lush and opulent as the rest of the facility. The tables were decorated in white linen with sterling silver accents. Crystal goblets filled with iced lemon water dotted every table, most of which were already filled with diners.

A waitress led me toward the far end of the room. A chatty little thing, she informed me of the prime real estate on which my table was located.

"Next to a window overlooking the grounds and one of the more private spots in the dining room. People often request the tables along that wall. I'm glad you planned ahead."

"A friend arranged this for me."

"How nice. Your friend thought of everything. Here we are. Have a seat. You'll be having a dining partner. I hope you don't mind. We are completely full this weekend. It's busy because of the large golf tournament on the grounds." She twinkled at me. "Spouses come along and enjoy the spa while their partners are golfing. It keeps everyone happy."

I knew that *I* was happy. I felt a little teary knowing that Molly, in spite of all her troubles with her traitorous brother, had arranged this beautiful gift for me. She is the most generous soul I've ever met. My hand shook with emotion as I reached for my water glass.

Then the waitress handed me a note addressed to me, in Molly's distinctive hand.

"I was asked to give you this. Have a nice dinner." And she sped away.

More from Molly? How could there possibly be more?

I slipped the notepaper from the envelope and opened it.

*Sammi,*
*Forgive me, please, for what I have done.*

So like Molly to think she'd "done" something, to take responsibility for everything.

*I want you to know Jared like I do. He is a wonderful man and a great big brother. It would make me so happy if I knew the two of you could get along—my new friend and my "old" big brother. I'm sorry about this, but I just couldn't think of another way to get you two together. Humor me, please?*
*And don't scare him off!*
*Molly*

Scare who off? I thought dully, my brain not functioning at full throttle.

Then I heard the waitress returning.

"And this is where you'll be sitting, sir. I hope you enjoy your meal."

I looked up with a smile on my face to greet my new dinner partner. The smile froze and shattered as I saw Jared Hamilton pull out the chair across from mine.

"You!"

He blinked and looked as dumbfounded and dismayed as I. "Sammi? Why…how…?" His forehead furrowed. "Molly strikes again."

"What does Molly have to do with you being here?" I demanded, a sinking sensation forming in my stomach. Surely Molly wouldn't subject me to her brother's presence intentionally.

"She sent me." He reached into his coat pocket and pulled out an exact duplicate of the card I had received. "The little scamp said it was my birthday present and I was so cranky these days I needed to go *immediately*."

"But why? If she sent me…she knows how I feel about…" I stopped just in time.

"About me? I'm sure you've told her often enough." There was a hint of irritation in his voice. Then he read his note and began to look genuinely puzzled. "I don't see why…"

"She must have planned this before you *fired* her," I said peevishly.

Jared stared at the card and shook his head. "No, she gave it to me after I fired her."

"But why?"

"As a way of telling me she understood."

"Then she understands more than I do!" I blurted, furious. "She is the sweetest, most generous, caring person…"

"I know all that," Jared said wearily. "I've lived with her my entire life."

"And you still had it in you to let her go? What does that make you?" I might have continued but at that moment a waitress came to the table with our lunch, a lovely piece of steamed salmon, an imaginatively arrayed bouquet of vegetables and a fruit bowl that looked like it had been arranged by a sculptor.

"Enjoy your meals."

We both stared down at the food and then up at each other. I'd like to say that my righteous indignation won out and I stormed away from the table and out of the spa altogether, but I didn't. The food and my appetite prevailed. There was no way I was going to let this guy chase me away from a perfectly divine meal. Apparently the food won Jared over, too, because he didn't appear any more willing to give up his spot than I was mine.

Finally, something we have in common—we're both too stubborn for our own good.

I put my hands in my lap and prayed the most unappreciative table grace of my life.

*Oh, Lord, thank You for this beautiful food, this wonderful place and the sweet friendship of Molly. Now, Lord, if it's in Your will, is there any way You can get this brother of hers off my back?*

When I raised my head, I realized that Jared was saying grace as well and surmised that his words were probably very close to mine. What would God do in a case like this? When both parties are praying to get rid of each other?

"Why…" I began.

"I don't know," he retorted.

"What was she thinking?"

"Molly doesn't think. She acts. Rashly."

For once I had to agree with him.

"What can we do?"

He looked at me, considering his answer. "Eat?" he finally ventured.

*Oh, why not.*

I picked up my fork. I wasn't about to let the likes of Jared Hamilton ruin my appetite.

I escaped to my room after our silent, uncomfortable meal. I needed to think. Why had Molly sent Jared here? The man fired her—she should have been furious with him. She wasn't rational, thinking Jared and I could become friends. Poor Molly is on the verge of a nervous breakdown. She's a French fry short of an order, a crayon short of a box. That had to be it, she was suffering an emotional collapse. Friends? Jared and me? When lions lie down with lambs, maybe.

More determined than ever not to let Jared's presence ruin my good time and vowing to encourage Molly to see a physician when I got home, I put on shorts and a T-shirt, grabbed my swimsuit, flip-flops and fluffy robe and headed for the spa treatment area.

The treatment area is as elegant as the public areas in the spa. The tiles on the floor run down the halls to treatment rooms and halfway up the walls. They are large, thick, earthy looking and warm to the touch, signaling that they are heated from beneath. I gave my name to the woman at the large round desk. She looked on her list, nodded and gestured toward overstuffed sofas nearby to wait my turn.

I sat down and lay back against the cushions with my eyes closed. Ecstasy! I didn't have to worry about another thing—including making decisions—until I returned home. Then raised, anxious voices intruded upon my reverie. It was workmen and spa employees in conversation.

"What do you mean, there's no water on the other side? There *has* to be water We can't run a spa without water!"

"Sorry, but a pipe has broken under the floor in the men's whirlpool area. We turned off all the water to that area. Plumbers are coming but we're going to have to do some excavating to find exactly where the leak is. That means ripping up the tile, fixing the break, laying a new subfloor and retiling."

"How long is this supposed to take?" It sounded like Olga speaking.

"It will take as long as it takes. Don't plan on using the men's side of the spa until noon tomorrow at the very earliest."

"Are you out of your mind? Do you know how much people pay to stay here? We can't tell them 'Sorry, we're closed,' just like that."

"The women's spa is plenty big. Don't you have spare rooms over here?"

"The men's and women's spas are separate for a reason. Privacy."

"Before you added on, wasn't that area used for everyone?"

"Yes, but we had a dividing wall in place then."

"So put up another one. Close off some of the rooms so they can be used by the men."

There was a long silence. "It wouldn't be my first choice, but it might work. Most of our guests are ladies this weekend since most of the gentlemen are out on the golf course during the day. There are some facilities that could be shared, I suppose."

"We can make a wall, but we can't prevent sound from crossing back and forth. It wouldn't be very private."

"It will have to do," the voice with the most authority said. "Get someone in here right now to put up some dividers. Now."

I groaned inwardly. Great. There went the peace and quiet I'd been so looking forward to. But how bad could it be?

Quite bad, I realized that afternoon as I walked down the hall to have my legs waxed. The treatment rooms, though sealed with doors, were open at the top, like cubicles in an office. Although sound didn't carry much, it was definitely not as private as secure rooms would have been.

Oh, well, I wasn't planning to talk to anyone, anyway. Nothing was going to ruin this wonderful gift. Even having leg hair ripped from my body with hot wax wouldn't deter me.

By the time I reentered the hallway, the makeshift dividers

were in place and draped with curtains. If I hadn't known better, I would have assumed it was intentional all along.

A young woman trotted toward me with a worried expression on her pretty face.

"I'm so sorry," she began, "but due to some plumbing problems, we have to share the manicure and pedicure bays with the men's side." She must have seen my alarm. "You won't be able to see each other because there are thick curtains around each pedicure chair, but sound may travel...."

There was no use fussing about the inconvenience. It would be over soon enough.

"That's fine. I'm sure it won't be a problem."

The woman, relieved that I didn't complain, led me toward my next indulgence.

The luxurious pedicure chair looked like a throne. The heavily cushioned leather engulfed me as I scrambled into place. She turned on the massage mechanisim and rollers began to work the muscles in my back. Warm water was bubbling for me to sink my feet into and everything was in place for the manicure to follow. Then I caught a waft of almonds and vanilla. Aromatherapy, too.

"Do you care for a beverage? Pineapple juice? Apricot? Apple? No? Then I'll leave you for a few moments so you can relax and soak your feet before the pedicure."

I sank into the chair and waited to be pampered.

I must have dozed off as my feet steeped in the aromatic water they'd scattered with rose petals, because I was startled awake by a man's voice coming from the next bay.

"A manicure and a pedicure? She ordered me a pedicure? Surely there's some mistake."

"No, Mr. Hamilton, it says right here, very specifically, that you are to have a pedicure this hour. So, if you'd just like to put your feet in this water...."

"No, I don't want to… What's that stuff floating in it?"

"Rose petals."

"I might as well stick my feet in soda pop. Cross this off the list and give my sister a refund or something. She can use it to pay for her straightjacket, the one she's going to be wearing when someone in the medical community hears what she's done…."

"Oh, sir, I don't have authority. I'd have to go to the front desk. It might take a few minutes. They're having some trouble with…"

"I know, I know. 'The plumbing in the men's spa.'"

I clapped my hand over my mouth to stifle a giggle as I heard Jared say wearily, "Then let's just do it. I can see that stopping this charade my sister has dreamed up will be harder than just getting it over with." Then there was splashing and a little yelp from Jared as his back hit the massaging rollers installed in the chair.

"Do women actually *like* this stuff?" he muttered. "And what on earth is that *smell?*"

All grew silent as we steeped side-by-side in our own rosy brew. I didn't know if I should laugh or cry.

But, if I were completely honest, a part of me was wickedly enjoying his discomfort. Not one of my finer moments. Suddenly I was reminded of Luke 7, when a woman wet Christ's feet with her tears, wiped them with the hair of her head and anointed them. Perhaps Molly believed she was doing on act of atonement. Who was I to stand in the way of that? My attitude began to improve.

*Please make Jared grateful. I know Molly is trying to be good to him. Help him see her motives, not the awkwardness. And help me to be gracious as well. I'm sorry for my attitude toward him. I'm going to try to improve. Help me?*

As the procedures progressed, I didn't announce my

presence on the other side of the canvas wall. I was having far too much fun hearing Jared experience his first pedicure.

"Ouch! What are you doing? You're scrubbing awfully hard, aren't you?"

"Your first pedicure, Mr. Hamilton?"

"And my last. A manicure is one thing, but this… That tickles!" Splashing noises came from the other side of the trompe l'oeil-decorated canvas wall.

I couldn't help it. I burst out laughing.

There was a sudden and profound silence from Jared's space.

Finally Jared's voice came floating over the divide. "Sammi, is that you?"

"Yes. And although I can't imagine why she sent you here, the least you can do is be gracious about it."

"Gracious? They're making soup out of my feet and trying to asphyxiate me with weird smells. And—" he gave another yelp of protest "—don't *do* that, it tickles!"

## Chapter Seventeen

Best pedicure I've ever had, I thought later as I got ready for my facial. Definitely the most fun. Hearing Jared splash around in the foot bath, yelping every time the poor woman working on him tried to touch the soles of his feet made my mischievous heart sing.

I'm not a vengeful person by nature, and I do understand why Molly wants her brother and me to get along. She cares about both of us. Her world would be far easier if we didn't mix like oil and water when we were together. If Molly had been able to accept that, I doubt she would have had the madcap idea to send us on this hopeless trip to throw us together.

But Jared's presence isn't bothering me. Quite frankly, it wouldn't surprise me if, after that abortive pedicure disaster, he'd already packed up and left. I willed my lips not to twitch, but I couldn't help it. I was smiling like a ninny when I ran into him in the hall.

"What are you grinning about?" he said irately.

"Enjoy your pedicure?" I asked sweetly, truly surprised he hadn't already turned tail and run.

"Best thing that's happened to me all afternoon," he growled. "Unfortunately I mean that."

I tipped my head to one side, confused.

"Some crazed woman caught me in the hall wondering if I were her next *back-waxing* appointment."

My eyes practically bulged from my head in my effort to keep from laughing. "Were you?"

"I didn't stick around to find out."

I shrugged helplessly to show that I, too, was being swept along by the force of Molly's wave.

"I wish I hadn't fired her before. Then I could have fired her now," he muttered.

"If you'll excuse me," I said, trying to push by his large, athletic form. "I have a glycolic acid peel next. I'm going to be exfoliated."

"I certainly hope so," he mumbled irritably. "Sounds like something that should happen to Molly, too. Is it painful?" he added hopefully.

I found myself grinning. "Why don't you try it and find out?" In spite of myself, I had to give the man credit. He was clearly sticking this out not because he wanted to, but because he knew it was important to Molly. There was such a dichotomy in the dynamics between them. He could fire her, but he couldn't disappoint her by leaving the spa.

"Because," he said as he thrust what looked like a dance card at me, "she's got me scheduled down to the minute. Next, I have a facial! They tell me men have them here all the time. What does this face need with a facial, anyway?"

Not much, my errant brain replied. There was very little that could improve on Jared's blatant handsomeness.

"I'm sure I don't know." I felt a good mood rising within me. At some point during that hilarious pedicure, I'd realized I'd decided to relax and enjoy the weekend *because* Jared was

here rather than in spite of him. He'd provided good entertainment thus far.

"We might as well walk together," I suggested. "Since we
both have appointments for facials."

"I thought you were having a peel of some sort, like having
your skin ripped off, right?"

"Don't you wish. Sounds to me like we're having the same
thing done."

"Not me." He started to turn away.

"But you'll disappoint your sister."

He hesitated.

"And this will remove all your dead skin cells, fine lines
and wrinkles. You'll be a new man."

His eyes were slits when he looked at me. "What's wrong
with the old one?"

"Ah, let me count the ways." I slipped my arm into his and
steered him toward our next appointments.


I didn't see Jared again until supper, when we met at our
assigned table. The dining room had been dimmed and
candles lit. The golfers had come in from the course and were
having dinner with their pampered spouses. There was a
happy hum of muted conversations throughout the room.

There was, however, more of a miserable, wretched,
moaning grumble at our table.

For one thing, Jared and I had discovered something else
we had in common. We are both sensitive to glycolic acid and
had faces red as boiled beets. I, being fair, had gotten the worst
of it. The last time I'd been this red was the day I walked
across the stage to pick up my graduation diploma with four
feet of toilet tissue dragging from the heel of my shoe.

"The skin will grow back eventually, don't you think?" I
asked by way of starting a conversation. Were I with anyone

else—someone, for example, that I'd had a crush on—I might have felt embarrassed. Jared, however, had somehow become a comfort zone for me to be myself. After all, if I was a beet, he was at least a radish.

He leaned back in his chair and studied me. "Why are we doing this, Sammi? Why don't we both just pick up and go home?"

"Because we're having fun?" I ventured as I stirred sweetener into my iced tea.

"Your idea of fun is being tortured, poked, prodded, having acid thrown in your face and being forced to breathe noxious fumes? Excuse me, but you're loonier than my sister."

"Come on, admit it. This will make a great story to tell your friend Ethan."

"You think I'd ever admit this to Ethan? Are you kidding?"

"Afraid of jeopardizing your masculinity?" I teased.

"Not in the least. I'm very sure of my masculinity." He leaned forward and his gaze captured mine. "I make you nervous, don't I, Sammi?"

Unfortunately at that very second, a wave of anxiety shivered its way down my spine. He *did* make me nervous. And what made me more uneasy still was that this unexpected feeling that had nothing to do with Molly and everything to do with me.

Batting the thought away like a bug in lamplight, I retorted, "You're talking nonsense."

"Am I?" He shifted in his seat. "Then you won't mind spending the evening with me. I hear they have wonderful entertainment for the guests in the evening. Music, games, walks in the moonlight…"

Music and moonlight? Oh, no. I love M&M's—music and moonlight—the most vulnerable of my romantic weaknesses.

"Thanks for asking, but I'd better get to bed early. I'm

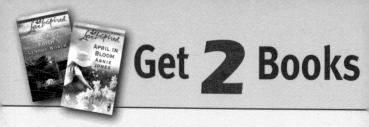

# Get 2 Books

## HOW TO GET YOUR
# 2 FREE BOOKS AND FREE GIFT

1. Peel off the 2 FREE BOOKS seal from the front cover. Place it in the space provided at right. This automatically entitles you to receive two free books and an exciting surprise gift.

2. Send back this card and you'll get 2 Love Inspired® books. These books have a combined cover price of $9.98 in the U.S. and $11.98 in Canada, but they are yours to keep absolutely FREE!

3. There's <u>no</u> catch. You're under <u>no</u> obligation to buy anything. We charge nothing – ZERO – for your first shipment. And you don't have to make any minimum number of purchases – not even one!

4. We call this line Love Inspired because each month you'll receive books that are filled with joy, faith and traditional values. The stories will lift your spirits and gladden your heart! You'll like the convenience of getting them delivered to your home well before they are in stores. And you'll love our discount prices, too!

5. We hope that after receiving your free books you'll want to remain a subscriber. But the choice is yours – to continue or cancel, anytime at all! So why not take us up on our invitation, with no risk of any kind. You'll be glad you did!

6. And remember…we'll send you a surprise gift ABSOLUTELY FREE just for giving Love Inspired novels a try!

### Steeple Hill®

## SPECIAL FREE GIFT!

We'll send you a fabulous surprise gift, absolutely FREE, simply for accepting our no-risk offer!

©2002 STEEPLE HILL BOOKS

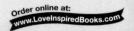

Order online at:
www.LoveInspiredBooks.com

# FREE!

**HURRY!** Return this card promptly to get 2 FREE books and a FREE gift!

Love Inspired.

**Yes,** please send me the 2 free Love Inspired® books and the FREE gift for which I qualify. I understand that I am under no obligation to purchase anything further, as explained on the opposite page.

affix
free
books
sticker
here

▼ DETACH AND MAIL CARD TODAY! ▼

(LI-CR-06)

313 IDL EE5E                    113 IDL EE5Q

| | |
|---|---|
| FIRST NAME | LAST NAME |

ADDRESS

| | |
|---|---|
| APT.# | CITY |

STATE/PROV.        ZIP/POSTAL CODE

Offer limited to one per household and not valid to current Love Inspired® book subscribers. All orders subject to approval. Books received may not be as shown. Credit or debit balances in a customer's account(s) may be offset by any other outstanding balance owed by or to the customer. Please allow 4 to 6 weeks for delivery.

## Steeple Hill Reader Service™—Here's How it Works:

Accepting your 2 free books and gift places you under no obligation to buy anything. You may keep the books and gift and return the shipping statement marked "cancel." If you do not cancel, about a month later we'll send you 4 additional books and bill you just $3.99 each in the U.S., or $4.74 each in Canada, plus 25¢ shipping & handling per book and applicable taxes if any.* That's the complete price, and — compared to cover prices of $4.99 each in the U.S. and $5.99 each in Canada — it's quite a bargain! You may cancel at any time, but if you choose to continue, every month we'll send you 4 more books, which you may either purchase at the discount price...or return to us and cancel your subscription.

*Terms and prices subject to change without notice. Sales tax applicable in N.Y.
Canadian residents will be charged applicable provincial taxes and GST.

If offer card is missing write to: Steeple Hill Reader Service, 3010 Walden Ave., P.O. Box 1867, Buffalo, NY 14240-1867

BUSINESS REPLY MAIL
FIRST-CLASS MAIL    PERMIT NO. 717-003    BUFFALO NY

POSTAGE WILL BE PAID BY ADDRESSEE

STEEPLE HILL READER SERVICE
3010 WALDEN AVE
PO BOX 1867
BUFFALO NY 14240-9952

NO POSTAGE
NECESSARY
IF MAILED
IN THE
UNITED STATES

scheduled for aerobics and a session with a weight trainer in the morning."

"Me, too. Molly probably planned it that way. She obviously wants us to kiss and make up, so why don't we oblige her?"

Just when I thought my cheeks couldn't get any redder, they did. *Kiss* and make up?

"So to speak. Come on, Sammi. I dare you." His eyes glittered as he leaned so close I could feel his breath on my cheek.

*Dare.* A challenge. Another Achilles' heel. One of these days I'm going to pay dearly for my pride and deserve every bit of it.

"Shall we?" Jared offered me his arm and nodded toward the grounds bathed in moonlight. The walks were lit by unobtrusive path lamps, and the bullfrogs and cicada were warming up their band. I was dizzy from the fragrance of freshly trimmed grass and floral scents I couldn't name.

"Oh, why not?" I said brightly. For being with a man I didn't like, I was certainly having difficulty fending off his charms. But it was only for tonight. Reality and tomorrow would come soon enough.

We walked a long time without speaking. Our steps matched perfectly, one benefit of being a tall woman paired with a tall man. For once I felt practically petite in comparison to my escort. I'm often told I have the build of a model. It's not all its cracked up to be. Being tall and long-legged sometimes makes it hard to find a date that I don't tower over. Especially in high heels.

The beauty of the night and the grounds was staggering in its perfection. It was almost as if I had spoken my own thoughts when Jared said, "God really knew what He was doing, didn't He?"

Though Molly had told me that Jared was a Christian, this statement still surprised me. I'm not sure what I expected of him. I suppose in my own mind, I'd become both judge and jury concerning him. *Shame on me.*

Still, I blurted, "Do you believe He's a God of compassion and mercy?"

"Yes. And justice, too." He paused by a large oak.

"Jared, there's something I have to ask you." My mouth went dry and the wings of the butterflies in my stomach were large as palm leaves.

"Hmm." He led me toward a wooden-platform swing tucked beneath the tree. In front of it was a small pond lit from beneath. I could see the koi resting near the bottom. He settled me in it as tenderly as if I were a child before dropping down beside me. We sat there, gently moving back and forth, sharing an innate rhythm.

Finally he spoke. "What question might that be?"

"If you are a Christian and if you love your sister, how could you fire her? I see such affection and respect between the two of you on one hand and such frustration and anger on the other. If what you say is true, how could you treat your sister this way? *Firing* her from her own business? Putting her out—" I snapped my newly polished fingers "—just like that."

"'Just like that'?" He frowned, but I saw genuine sadness in his expression. "You think it was easy, then?"

"No. It couldn't have been easy. Molly respects and admires you. She *loves* you. Help me to understand."

He was silent so long that I was terrified I'd offended him and ruined this new, sweet truce between us.

Finally, he spoke. "I fired Molly because she asked me to."

Shock made me sit bolt upright. "What?"

I could see him shake his head and scrape his fingers through his hair, the signal of his greatest agitation. "Molly did something at the office…*to* the office…that I found unconscionable. I let my anger get the best of me, I'm afraid. God forgive me. I've regretted it ever since, but there was no way I could pull back my words. In my rage, I told her that if she were anyone else, I would have fired her on the spot. That I *should* fire her. That if she didn't get her messes straightened out, I *would* fire her. I regretted it immediately but there was no way I could take it back."

I stiffened. What was he saying?

"Molly, being Molly, jumped on it. She said she *wanted* me to fire her. That it would be best all-around." His breath caught in his throat. "She knew I was angry. She also knew why I was angry. She demanded that I tell people what she'd done and then fire her."

I'd tipped over and fallen through the looking glass were everything was topsy-turvy. "I don't understand."

Jared pulled an envelope from out of his pocket and handed it to me. "I'd forgotten this was in my jacket until I noticed it while I was dressing. Maybe it's for the best. You can read the instigating message for yourself."

I opened the envelope and pulled out the impressive letterhead. I leaned forward to read it in the dim lamplight.

…I am sorry to inform you that I have chosen not to use the services of Hamilton and Hamilton. Although your firm has a sterling reputation, I am inclined to place significant weight on first impressions. The somewhat confusing presentation given to me by Ms. Hamilton leads me to question the organizational abilities of your company. As I indicated in our phone conversation, Ms. Hamilton came to the presentation unprepared or, at least, without notes and the promised support materials which she had apparently forgotten at her office.

It is with regret that I must inform you of this. You were recommended to me by someone I regard highly and, although I found your partner delightful as a

person, she appears unable to keep track of a large port-
folio such as my own.

A word of warning: I have heard through the business
grapevine of other instances in which Ms. Hamilton
"dropped the ball," so to speak. You might want to look
at the effect that is having on your office's reputation.

"I didn't want anyone to know what had happened. Neither
did I want it to reflect badly on Molly. She's a smart woman
with glaring weaknesses that she can't seem to overcome. She
knew I wouldn't announce to the world that she'd made a
blunder, so she decided to help me. At our staff meeting she
made it known to one and all that she'd been fired."

*What?*

"How was I supposed to sort *that* out? It couldn't be done
right there, in front of everyone. Her reputation would have
been ruined. So I played along. I told them that I would fire
Molly if she made another error—and I refused to say what
the error was—but that I was giving her one more chance to
redeem herself and that everyone would have to trust me to
decide if Molly were to stay in the company or not.

"She was furious with me. She'd hoped she'd maneuvered
me into a corner and had trapped me into letting her go. She
knew I wouldn't let her quit, that even if she didn't come to
work, I'd still send her a paycheck, and so she tried to make
the problem public."

"I don't get it, Jared."

He looked at me fixedly and I could see the intensity in his
eyes. "That's because that's where you came in—as Molly's
'second chance.'"

"Me?"

"It's why Ethan introduced us and why I hired you. I didn't
want to fire Molly. I wanted her to get her act together. And

I didn't want anyone to know the kind of blunders she'd made. I wanted to protect her. But her self-esteem has dropped to such a desperate low that I believe she was *trying* to get me to punish her." There was a catch in his voice as he added, "And now, it seems, she's·succeeded."

My mind wasn't agile enough to comprehend all he was saying. Still, there was one refrain that seemed stuck on a loop in my mind. *He isn't the bad guy after all. He isn't the bad guy. He isn't the bad guy.*

So if Jared Hamilton isn't the bad guy, who is he?

## Chapter Eighteen

"What on earth could she have done that was so awful? And why is her self-esteem so low? She's smart, attractive charming, funny…" I caught myself before adding, *just like you.*

"First, I'd like you to understand how it is with Molly, how it's always been." I saw him run his tongue over his lower lip as he took a breath. Always, it seems, he has difficulty talking about Molly.

"I was the happiest little boy in the world when Molly was born. I'd wanted a sibling my entire short life. I'd wanted someone 'of my own' to play with and reasoned that my parents had brought her into the family just for me." He frowned. "It wasn't long before I realized that Molly was in our family because there were three of us to raise her instead of just two.

"Molly, as a child, was a full-time job. She had the attention span of a flea. She was impossible to teach new games to—they were all too slow moving for her. She wet the bed and she wriggled and squirmed almost constantly. She always acted before she thought and couldn't sit still if her life depended on it. She was bright as a whip but still had a hard time in school, mostly because she didn't pay attention. She drove my parents wild."

He sighed. "I spent most of my time bailing her out of difficulties of her own making. She would do things impulsively and I'd have to undo them. Even now, she's usually late for appointments and, while she's always enthusiastic about everything she does, she has a difficult time getting projects finished. But because she functioned well in the banking world with all its rules and regulations, I thought that working with me would be a piece of cake for her.

"Molly has never had much self-esteem. She knows she's not living up to her potential and she hates herself for it. She's convinced herself that she's too big a burden for me. Since I don't see it that way, she's trying to force me to deal with her like I would any other employee who'd done what she did."

"Jared, you keep talking like this 'thing' Molly did is irreparable. No one has died over it, have they?"

He chuckled. "Not that I know of."

"Then what could be so bad?"

I heard him shift in place, as if the swing were suddenly too small for him.

"I wanted Molly to succeed and I wanted her to gain some self-esteem. I thought the way that might happen would be to trust her with a couple of large accounts. There's nothing wrong with her mind, only her self-discipline. She assured me that she was up to it, so I turned two important accounts over to her."

"And?" I felt a sinking sensation in my stomach. This story seemed to be heading to a very bad end.

"And she lost both accounts at the presentation stage. She came without her materials to one and showed up a day late for the other. Said she'd gotten it 'confused' in her calendar."

Uh-oh.

"It was, of course, a mistake which cost us two very important clients."

I closed my eyes and imagined how devastated Molly must have been—and Jared.

"Molly overheard one of them tell me that they'd consider coming back when I removed her from the business."

"But could it have been *so* bad? Surely she wouldn't let it happen again."

"It scared Molly. She had no excuse for her behavior other than to say that she'd lost her files in her 'mess.' What has troubled her more was the loss of the money these clients would have brought to our company."

"How much could it be?" I stammered. "Surely it could be made up…."

"Let's just say, over a ten-year period it could potentially add up to a million or more dollars."

My jaw dropped and hung there. I was speechless.

"You see, don't you, why I was angry with her? First, because she nearly brought Hamilton and Hamilton to its knees, and second, because she's been absolutely pigheaded about not believing that she can still remain in the company." He looked into my eyes, and, even in the dimness of lamplight, I could see his pain. "She really pushed me, Sammi. Hard. She made me angry with her for her behavior about the mistake, not the mistake itself.

"And that's when you came into the picture. I was furious for all sorts of reasons yet still ready to play the big brother and attempt to protect her from herself. Molly was contrite, penitent and completely unwilling to see reason or to forgive herself. I know it doesn't make much sense, but you haven't lived with Molly as long as I have. There's not a lot about her that *does* make sense sometimes.

"Yes, I was furious with her. Yes, she did make me want to fire her. And, yes, I did finally do what she wanted. She's bent on paying some kind of penance and thinks this is the only way to do it."

He sank back against the swing and we rocked a little harder.

"You figure it out," he finally said, his voice muffled. "I certainly can't."

I felt, rather than heard, him sigh, and experienced a wave of shame overtake me.

*Lord, You certainly do know how to point out my shortcomings, don't You? Every time I see and acknowledge a weakness and turn it over to You, You shine Your light on another even more glaring flaw. Every time I experience this I wonder how it is You tolerate us frail, imperfect children of Yours. I have been unjustly judgmental about Jared and believed I was so righteous about his behavior toward his sister. Now I see that I knew nothing about their relationship or Jared as a man. I'm so ashamed. Forgive me.*

And God was not the only one to whom I needed to apologize.

"Jared?"

"Hmmm?" He was gazing up at the stars.

"Will you forgive me?"

I felt him turn toward me in the darkness.

"For what?"

"For being a self-righteous, smug, holier-than-thou, judgmental snob."

The swing shook a little as he chuckled. "For all that?"

"I have been completely off-base concerning your relationship with Molly. I thought you were bad-tempered, hardhearted, egotistical, selfish and without feeling." Tears began to pool behind my eyes and I choked on my words. "Now, when it's too late, I realize you are loving and caring toward your sister and have never desired anything but the best for her. I am so sorry."

If, at that moment, I could have disappeared into the ground, I gladly would have. What a brat I'd been in my attitude toward him! Would I ever learn?

"What do you mean, 'too late'?" came the amused question out of the darkness. "It's not too late for Molly and me. We love each other. We've fought this battle over our vast differences before and we'll fight it again. Just because she drives me crazy doesn't mean I don't love her. 'Love conquers all,' right?"

He leaned forward and his face was partially lit by the lights on the walking path. "And I'd like to think it's just beginning for us, Sammi. We got off to a lousy start. What would you say to a fresh one?"

"I…you mean you would…you still…" I blubbered into the crisp white handkerchief he gave me and blew my nose until I sounded like a honking goose. Lovely. When I finally take a look at my shortcomings, they are all over the map.

He unfolded from the swing, drew himself to his full, imposing height and stretched out his hand to me. "Ms. Smith? My name is Jared Hamilton. I'm so pleased to finally meet you. I've heard so many good things about you from my sister."

A grin tweaked the corners of my mouth. I stood, too, stretching up to *my* full height and was still able to tilt my head upward to look at him. "Mr. Hamilton, charmed, I'm sure. Your sister says wonderful things about you, as well. I'm so glad to finally meet you."

*The real you.*

"I hope you don't think I'm too forward, but since I already feel like I've known you for a very long time, I was wondering if you'd like to go to the main spa facility and listen to the musical trio that's playing there."

I laid my hand in his and the warmth and strength of his palm filled me with a sense of security and delight. "Mr. Hamilton, your sister never mentioned what a charmer you are."

His teeth flashed white in the moonlight. "Good. That's something I'd like to show you myself."

The clubhouse was filled with light and music. Although I'm not sure the staff was telling the truth, they insisted that the dessert buffet they served was absolutely low calorie. I, with my highly efficient metabolism, took them at their word and ate double just to make sure I didn't fade away before morning.

If this is a movie, then I'm the star, I thought as I drifted in a giddy haze through the rest of the evening. I felt beautiful. More accurately, Jared made me feel beautiful. On the inside, where it counts. He also made me feel smart, witty, wise, exuberant, calm, excited, happy…

What had happened to bat-man, the grouchy creature hovering in the corner of Ethan Carver's office? No wonder he'd been upset. Molly had spun him into a tizzy. I'd met him on a doubly awful day, with a crisis on each of the sibling and financial fronts. Thinking back now, I realize that he was probably actually pretty *nice* considering what he'd been going through.

I watched him moving across the floor to me carrying another plate of food—if one could call it that. But it didn't matter that all the food on the plate didn't add up to eight total calories because the guy carrying it was yummy enough to count as a double fudge chocolate cake.

I felt a tightening in my chest as he came nearer. It wasn't supposed to be like this. Love wasn't supposed to happen so fast—not, at least, by my definition. I've always believed that love could be planned, sketched out in a day-timer, so to speak. First came casual coffee meetings, then a lunch or two. After that came dinner, movies, long walks in the park. When I met the man I would fall in love with, I was sure it would follow a formal, proper sort of path of getting to know and trust each other, taking each other to church and to meet our families. Then, and only then, would we know each other well enough to allow ourselves to fall in love.

At least that's the way I had it figured until I met Jared.

The path got turned on its head with him. First I disliked and mistrusted him. Then came resentment, frustration and anger. I was furious with him, didn't understand him and wished him out of my life. And *then,* almost overnight, I fell in love with him.

This was definitely not the way this organizational planner would have designed it.

Then he came near, leaned down and put a gentle kiss on my forehead and all sensible planning went out the window.

I looked for Jared at breakfast, but he didn't come to the dining room. I was amazed to realize how disappointed I felt not to see him.

It had been late when we'd finally said good-night, but Jared hardly seemed like the kind of person who'd be sleeping in on a morning like this….

Then I saw him coming across the room. He was wearing low-slung denim jeans and a soft white cotton shirt that stretched across his muscular chest. His hair was wet and raggedly slicked away from his face and he had a white towel draped around his neck. When he neared, I smelled the faint hint of chlorine from the pool.

"So that's where you've been." I beamed at him like a lighthouse. What had ever made me think he was mean and cantankerous? Then my logical mind reminded me that he *had* been bad-tempered. But I'd been perfectly happy to believe that was the sum of him. *Lord, You do have ways of opening a person's eyes!*

"Water's great. You should try it."

"I might. If I have time, that is. Molly signed me up for another full day." I pushed my schedule toward him.

| 10:00 a.m. | —Green Tea and Lime Leaf Exfoliating Body Scrub |
| 11:00 a.m. | —Sole Revival—Reflexology |
| 12:00 noon | —Lunch |
| 1:00 p.m. | —Body Wrap |
| 3:00 p.m. | —Full Body Massage |
| 5:00 p.m. | —Appetizers served in lounge |
| 6:00 p.m. | —Dinner |
| 8:00 p.m. | —Lecture in the Grecian room |

Tonight's subject: The Art of Romance

He read it and his eyebrow lifted quizzically. "Odd, but my schedule is exactly the same as yours. Do you think my sister was counting on the two of us running into each other a few times over the weekend?"

"We've underestimated her, Jared. She may appear disorganized, but when she sets her mind to it…"

"I've been handling Molly all wrong. I should have hired her an assistant at the start and just let her be an idea person. 'The Art of Romance'? Not too subtle, is she?"

"Like a Mack truck on an open highway."

Jared took my hand and grinned. "I'll have to tell her how much I love that quality in her when I get home."

# Chapter Nineteen

Despite all Molly's scheming to throw Jared and me together, even she couldn't have planned the bit about the plumbing. That was the unintentional crowning touch in Molly's little design.

The receptionist in the spa area looked up with a worried expression as I entered, ready and eager to be turned into a summer beverage by my green tea and lime leaf body treatment.

"The plumbing isn't fixed yet," she apologized. "We have you scheduled at the same time as one of our male guests. We'll have to use adjoining treatment areas. We will make sure you don't cross in the hallway but if that's a problem…"

Nothing was a problem to me right now. After last night with Jared, I was floating slightly above the ground on my own little happy cloud. I waved my hand dismissively. I could share the building with an ice floe full of polar bears and not mind today.

As I walked toward my appointment, I heard a loud complaint. Someone had gotten here before me.

"That stuff smells like a Chinese restaurant…I don't care how much it costs," the familiar voice roared. "I'll pay you double to take it away!"

Jared's take on these relaxing ablutions was quite different from mine, I thought as I tried to snuff out the grin spreading across my face.

I really don't know how much money he had forked out by the end of the morning, but I did hear him offer a hundred dollars to the reflexologist if she would just leave his feet alone.

The full body wrap that afternoon was much like being wrapped in warm, wet canvas and steeped like a minty organic tea bag until every toxin, even those hanging on for dear life, was sucked up and out of my body.

I recognized when Jared entered the treatment room on the other side of the wall by his incessant patter of questions.

"What's that smell? Why is it so steamy in here? Did you graduate from the Spanish inquisition Spa School, too? Whaddayamean you're going to wrap me up in sheets? I'm not a cabbage roll, you know."

Even now that I'd fallen head over heels for him, I couldn't help smiling. There's something so helpless and absurd about a tough-guy businessman being subjected to the mysterious world of pampering and relaxation.

There's also something rather pathetic about that same man pleading to have his arms unwrapped so he didn't feel like King Tut about to be placed in his sarcophagus.

By the time I was done with my massage later that afternoon, I was so relaxed that my legs were soft rubber. I groped my way to my room and collapsed across the bed. I don't believe I even twitched before I fell asleep.

I woke up at five, still in the rag-doll position I'd fallen in. There was a pool of drool on the pillow by my mouth and I had to lift my eyelids with my index finger. Now *that's* a sound sleep.

My phone rang as I finished putting on my makeup. It was

a jarring sound in my tranquil cloud. I wanted to ignore it but I'm far too snoopy to do that.

"Hello?"

"Sammi? How is it?" Molly sounded like a child with a new toy. "Is it wonderful?"

"Yes, it is, you sneaky thing, you! Bliss!"

"Are you mad at me?"

"Let's just say it's a good thing you weren't here when I discovered that your brother also checked in for the weekend."

"And now?" Her voice practically quivered with hope.

"You were right and I was wrong. He's a gem, Molly."

She chortled with delight. "I told you so! Isn't he just the best?"

"The best."

"Are you friends now?"

*More than!*

"Yes, dear. Mission accomplished."

I could practically feel her lean back with a satisfied sigh. Then she seemed to think better of relaxing quite yet. "How's Jared feeling about this?"

I thought about last night and grinned to myself. "Fine and dandy, I believe."

"I love it! I shouldn't have called and interrupted you, but I had to know. One of my friends invited me to her lake cabin for the week and I won't be here when you get back. Now I can go to the lake happy, content that the two of you finally got to know each other without me in the middle, confusing matters."

"You don't confuse me, Molly." Something had occurred to me this morning that might actually clear up some confusion. "In fact, I've been thinking about you a lot the past couple days. About why you've had such a hard time at Hamilton and Hamilton…"

"That can wait, Sammi. When I get back on Thursday I

want to hear everything." She sounded breathless and in high spirits. "I see my ride pulling up. Tell Jared 'hi' and that I'd planned to call him but, as usual, I've run out of time. Give him a kiss for me, will you?"

*Gladly.*

"You're the greatest, Sammi."

I felt tears scratch the backs of my eye. "And you're pretty terrific yourself, Molly. Now go have fun."

She hung up, and the dial tone hummed in my ear.

*Thank You, Lord, for the gift of friendship. My cup overflows. It is shaken down and spilling over in my life now that I know Molly and Jared.*

What more could I want? I thought, as I smoothed my hair into a soft wave that fell across one eye. It feels as though I already have it all and…yet…the part of me that wants my world in order, loves planning and mistrusts impulse is agitating within me. It's the strong, vocal part of me that always says, "Better safe than sorry, Sammi" and "Plan ahead." It's the same part of me, of course, that reminds me that Barbie was a fool to let go of a steady, reliable guy like Ken, that tells me that following my heart might lead me into disaster.

And now I've fallen in love…in the short space of a weekend…with my former client's brother…whom I disliked intensely only forty-eight hours ago. This is totally out of character for me, as foreign a language to me as Swahili.

It's almost too much for a pragmatic, cool-headed Scandinavian girl to bear.

"There you are!" Jared waited for me by the door, and by the way his eyes lit up when I walked in, I knew he was overjoyed to see me.

What an amazing turnaround it had been for us in the last few hours. We'd not only made peace with each other, we were buzzing around each other like two bugs drawn to each other's light. Molly's idea was inspired. If we could send all our world leaders to a spa for a month or two, they'd be so mellow we could get things like world peace worked out and have time left over for a facial.

As his fingers touched my elbow and he cradled my arm in his hand, a sense of *rightness* washed over me like a blessing. It was a rightness I'd never felt with anyone else in my life.

*Is he the one for me, Lord? Now? When I was least expecting it?*

Isn't that the way with God? He's a Father who loves to surprise us with gifts far more wonderful than we could ever expect or design for ourselves. I looked up and into Jared's eyes—a gift in itself for someone my height—and saw my feelings mirrored there.

For a person who is risk-averse like me, who likes preplanning and loves caution, this is a brand-new experience. Prudence was replaced by infatuation as I drifted through dinner in a delirious haze. Cardboard would have tasted divine. I could have been eating chicken lips and fish eyebrows and loved it all. And what made it all the more wonderful was that Jared seemed to share my happiness.

"I certainly underestimated you," I admitted. "I was sure your heart was made of stone—or ice—and now…"

"Molly says it's my biggest flaw—being too soft with her." His voice softened.

"That reminds me. She called. I'm supposed to tell you 'hi.' She'd planned to call you as well but was running late, and her ride came. Apparently she is headed to a friend's lake cabin."

"She called you?" He seemed surprised.

"She wanted to know if I'd learned to like her big brother as much as she does."

His eyes twinkled. "And?"

"As much. Maybe even more."

"Imagine that." His voice softened and the way he looked at me made my heart leap in my chest.

"And she told me to give you this." I leaned forward and placed a gentle kiss on his cheek.

"Now I have even more to thank her for." He shook his head and I saw sadness creep into his expression. "Sometimes she just breaks my heart."

What a strange thing to say!

"You haven't heard any of the Molly stories, have you?" he asked ruefully.

"What do you mean?"

"Molly, the Lake and the Mislaid Car, Molly and the Missing Children, Molly and the Mystery of the Lost Purse, Vanishing Graduation Diploma and Straying Lawn Mower?" He sighed and leaned back in his chair as if this might take a long, long time.

"Sounds better than a Nancy Drew series," I commented. "Tell me more."

"When Molly was sixteen, my father bought her a car. Nothing fancy. A used Cavalier. Granted, it wasn't much of a car, small and inexpensive, but it got good gas mileage. Molly was only supposed to drive it to specified places like school, the park near home and to a few reliable friends' homes.

"My sister has always been…distracted. She's always thinking ahead and sometimes forgets to live in the present. Anyway, she and her friends decided to have an afternoon birthday party for one of the girls in her group and hold it at the park. It's pretty there, a nice little lake, more of a pond, really, shelters, fire pits, the works.

"Molly, as usual, volunteered to do about seven things, including decorations, the cake, start the fire…well, you get the idea."

I nodded. I could just see her bustling around, trying to make things nice for the birthday girl.

"She went early, of course, so by the time the other girls arrived, she had everything ready. Apparently they had a good time, because it was early evening when the party began to break up. Molly was taking down the decorations when one of the girls asked her if she needed a ride home.

"Of course, Molly said she'd driven herself and turned to point to her car. That's the first anyone noticed that the car was missing."

"Stolen?" I gasped. "Poor kid!"

"Not exactly. The police and my parents were called. It was the first officer to arrive to take down a description of the car who noticed the rear bumper of a red Cavalier jutting out of the lake just below the girls' campsite."

I clamped a hand over my mouth to keep my jaw from dropping.

Jared looked both weary and amused as he said, "Close as anyone can figure, Molly drove to the shelter, unloaded the decorations and cake and then parked the car. Unfortunately she parked the car close to the lake in a spot where the ground falls fairly steeply toward the water. There's no real shore there and there's a drop-off. That, combined with the fact that Molly turned off the ignition without shifting the car into Park or Neutral, made it easy for the car to roll into the water."

I suddenly felt much of Jared's weariness—and no little portion of his amusement, as well.

"The girls admitted to having a boom box on full blast so no one heard a thing when the car rolled into the water."

"What did your parents…the police…" I heard myself stammering.

"They called someone to retrieve the car, but no one even scolded Molly. She took care of that herself."

He smiled at my quizzical gaze. "She grounded herself for
three months, took away all her own dating privileges and
promised to get a job to pay for having the car refurbished."

"That's harsh."

"She's always harsh with herself. Far worse than my
parents would have been. I think she's so disappointed with
herself sometimes that whatever punishment she metes out is
more painful than anyone else would ever dream up."

"So did she do all those things?"

"My parents made her pay for the car. The rest they didn't
press. Nobody wants Molly miserable—except Molly." Jared
chuckled. "She told everyone from then on that she was on
probation and that they should all hide their keys when she
came around."

"Well, it was just a one-time incident." I looked into Jared's
eyes. "Wasn't it?"

"Not exactly. There's also the story of Molly and the Lost
Car at the Airport Parking Lot and dozens of Molly and the
Missing Keys stories."

"Well, at least that was the worst of it."

"Not exactly." Jared played with his spoon, tapping it on
the water glass, the centerpiece, his coffee cup. It was as
though thinking about these things made him nervous.

"What do you mean, 'not exactly'?"

"There was the time Molly lost some children."

"I'm not sure I want to hear this one."

"It has a happy ending."

"Okay, then."

"While she was babysitting for our neighbor, who has three
children, Molly got the brilliant idea that she would take the
kids into downtown Minneapolis to go Christmas shopping
for the children's mother. After that, just think major department store, lost children, chaos and panic."

I sometimes feel lost, chaotic and panicky when I'm Christmas shopping. I could hardly imagine Molly as a teenager with three little kids...

"Apparently, Molly got distracted by some jewelry and took her eyes off the children for a few moments."

"Quick. Tell me the happy ending."

"It didn't come quickly. She did have the presence of mind to ask for help immediately. They locked the doors and scoured every inch of the store."

"And the children?"

"It seemed that they'd vanished into thin air."

"Where did they find them?"

"In the last place they looked."

"Of course."

"The kids had found the door that leads to the outside display windows. It being Christmas, there was one entire scene of Santa's workshop, another of a line of children waiting to see Santa and a third of a family of kids waiting by the fire for Santa to arrive."

"And?"

"Apparently the children had crawled into the window displays and played there for quite some time, to the delight of the people on the sidewalk. If anyone had walked out the door and asked if three little kids had gone by, they would have found them immediately. By the time police got to them, however, one child had crawled into Santa's lap and was sound asleep, another had lain down on the floor with the mannequins of the children in repose waiting for Santa Claus and had fallen asleep with them. The third, the oldest, had gathered all the loose toys from the elves at the workshop and taken them behind a curtain to play with them. He had made a Lincoln log house, a fort of blocks and was putting the finishing touches on a Lego airport when they found him."

"And Molly?"

"She'd sworn herself to a life of chastity, bread and water and no makeup for a month by the time we got there. She also offered to give up television, the phone in her room, popcorn and chocolate. She was trying to think up a worse punishment, but she hadn't yet been able to commit herself to an entire lifetime without mascara and blush."

I laughed, because Jared made it sound so funny, but I saw that Molly's external clutter and chaos had much to do with her internal goings-on. Before I could speak, Jared leaned forward and put his hand over mine, and I felt a zing of energy bolt up my arm like lightning. It knocked out all my power receptors, and I was putty in his hands.

"Enough about Molly. More about you."

And I was almost sure he added under his breath, "And me."

We'd been talking for some time, utterly unaware of everything around us when I remembered the thought that had come into my head earlier.

"Jared, do you think it's possible that Molly has ADD?"

"Attention Deficit Disorder? I doubt she's been evaluated. I'm not sure that twenty years ago people were quite so aware of it as they are now. Why?"

"Because it would explain so much of Molly's behavior."

Jared looked mildly interested. "Really? I don't know much about it, other than it seems to be in the news a lot these days."

"I'm no specialist, but I have a cousin whose daughter has ADD. In fact, I feel rather stupid that I didn't consider this before now. I'd assumed it had been ruled out in Molly's case, but she has all the signs."

"Such as?" He was twirling a lock of my hair with his index finger and not paying much attention to what I was saying.

I was having difficulty paying attention to what I was saying, too, but I forged ahead. "Distractibility, a short attention span, bed wetting late into childhood, doesn't listen well to directions, misplaces things, is easily bored, restless, fidgety, can't sit still, impulsive, trouble with follow-through, inefficient…" The longer I talked, the more impact the symptoms had on my consciousness.

On Jared's, too, apparently. He straightened and let my curl fall from his finger. "You're describing Molly exactly."

"I don't know why I didn't think of it before, other than I don't usually think of ADD manifesting in adults. It has to, of course, but we hear so much about diagnosing it in children these days…"

Jared's forehead was wrinkled into a frown. "It makes sense. Perfect sense, in fact. I wish I knew more…." Then he shook himself like a big wet dog just out of a pond. "But we can discuss it later. Tonight—" and he touched the tip of his finger to my lips and drew it down the curve of my cheek "—is for us."

## *Chapter Twenty*

There was a string quartet playing in the Grecian room and a waiter glided around the room offering appetizers to those milling about. My stomach gave a great heave of hunger and I tried to catch his eye. Another waiter appeared and offered me my choice of beverage—water, bubbly or still, soda water with lemon or lime or something he called a "water beverage" flavored with fruit juice. Nice as this little soiree might be, we were still obviously at a health spa and they were elegantly attempting to force us to get in the required eight to ten glasses a day.

Although the appetizers weren't made of water, it was close—cucumbers with a sprig of dill, radish roses with a single caper as their center, carrot coins topped with a minuscule daub of something white—whipped cottage cheese, probably. There was caviar—three eggs per toast point—and one slice of bread had no doubt been enough to serve the entire room. My hunger nipped at my insides with the persistence of a termite on wood.

Jared walked over to me with a grin on his face. "What game are we playing here— the 'imagine there's food on the plates and pretend to eat it' game?"

"We're eating light."

"Huh. We're eating invisible. I picked up what someone called a watercress sandwich and held it to the light. I've seen paper thicker than that bread. This is like the story of the emperor's new clothes. Everyone's pretending to enjoy the food, and there's nothing on the plate."

I patted my stomach. "It will keep us trim."

Jared looked me up and down. "Let me see, a radiant Scandinavian ice princess who isn't wintry after all. Silvery blond hair, frosty blue eyes, a complexion perfect as porcelain…yes, I can see why you might worry if you put on a pound or two."

I felt a blush bleeding through my entire body. "You shouldn't…"

"Why not? It's true. So is the fact that you are graceful, move like a dancer and turn heads wherever you go."

He watched my expression turn to astonishment. "Of course, that's not why I like you."

My mouth worked like that of a fish out of water.

"I like you because you're funny, intelligent, independent and you don't let me get away with anything—even bullying my own sister."

Having been completely blindsided by this shower of accolades, I was glad for the waiter who came by to offer me an appetizer—a twig of celery with a minuscule speck of cream cheese spread on it.

Fortunately there was more substance to the rest of the evening than there was to the food.

"The Art of Romance" program turned out to be an eclectic mix of romantic paintings throughout history, romantic music, poetry and a few funky extras. One of these extras was a "Qualities of the Ideal Man" contest. Now, I'm not much on contests, but when first prize is a free night's stay at the Oasis, I can become pretty creative.

"You're going to do it?" Jared asked. "Write a list of what you want in a man?"

"This is for fun, you know. I don't think they expect something terribly deep or inspired." I was already recalling some of the ridiculous conversations Wendy and I had had about men over the years.

"Aren't you going to reveal your personal requirements?" He studied me with a soft smile. "Otherwise, how will I know how to act?" Jared put his hand over mine. "I don't want to disappoint you."

I leaned close to his ear and whispered, "Don't worry, I'll tutor you."

"I want to be teacher's pet."

"You already are." Then, so as to not draw any more attention to us, I grabbed the pen and paper I'd been given and started to create the requirements I figure most women want in their ideal man.

Jared, seeing I was serious, wandered off to learn how to read poetry and dip strawberries into chocolate, leaving me to my imagination.

### Qualities of an Ideal Man
### by Sammi Smith

1. He laughs at my jokes.
2. Showers regularly.
3. Understands PMS and its consequences, is unafraid of a woman in hormonal flux and knows that chocolate, flowers and jewelry are the only real cures despite what medical experts say.
4. Can read my mind.
5. Is willing to give up the remote without twitching, trying to hide it under a cushion or wanting to "discuss" why I want it.

6. Chews with his mouth closed.
7. Knows when to say "Yes, darling," and mean it.
8. Calls me when I'm thinking about him.
9. Calls me when I'm not thinking about him.
10. Just calls.
11. Remembers my birthday, the anniversary of the day we met and any other day I've decided in my mind is special (but have not even told him about—see quality #4—mind reading).
12. Owns candles and knows how to use them.
13. Thinks a week without bringing me flowers is a disgrace.
14. Says I'm the most beautiful woman on the planet—and means it (This has nothing to do with near-sightedness and everything to do with inner-sightedness).
15. Takes walks with me under the stars.
16. Know the right answer to the question "Does this make me look fat?"
17. Shares my spiritual beliefs.
18. Never lets a day pass without saying "I love you."

I turned in my list to the spa staff who were doubling as contest judges and went to find Jared.

"What happened to the chocolate-dipped berries?" I asked, mouth watering already.

"We ate them. Every guy here is starving, Sammi." He lowered his voice. "Someone went out on a covert run for pizzas. We're planning our rendezvous for later. I don't think the staff patrols the prison yard at night. If they do, we'll just have to make a break for it." His eyes grew wide and serious. "If I'm caught and they throw me in solitary confinement, tell Molly thanks anyway for the great weekend."

"Okay, drama king. And what else did you do while I was gone?"

"I discovered I really don't agree with Alfred, Lord Tennyson."

"Say what?"

"'Tis better to have loved and lost than never to have loved at all.'" He looked dreadfully serious all of a sudden as he took my hand. "I'm not sure I could stand to lose you now, Sammi, any more than I could bear to lose one of my family. I think it might be better to never love than to think of it slipping away from you."

*He was talking about me…us!* My heart should have, by rights, exploded in my chest, the way it was feeling. *Us!*

I opened my mouth to respond but at that moment someone rang the huge gong that sat in the foyer of the Oasis and the sound hung, shivering, in the air.

"The staff of the Oasis would like to thank you all for coming tonight, and before our party ends, we would like to present the winner of the Qualities of an Ideal Man contest with her prize. Ms. Samantha Smith, will you please come forward?"

Jared whooped and the others clapped as I slunk forward to pick up my prize. Then I straightened my shoulders and threw back my head. What was I embarrassed about? Not only could I describe a romantic man, I *had* one! Next time I came to the spa to use my gift certificate, I'd bring Molly with me—out of gratitude for forcing me to see exactly who and what her brother really is.

We strolled through the grounds holding hands and saying very little. I had neither the urge nor desire to break the comfortable silence between us. Jared, it seemed, didn't, either. Finally we settled on a wrought iron settee on the patio. The grounds grew quiet as the guests returned to their rooms for the night.

The moon hung like an opalescent disk, a brooch on navy velvet with a scattering of diamonds sparkling around it in the sky.

"What a night." He said it as if expecting no answer.

"A jewel of a night." *In more ways than one!*

"A marvel, certainly."

"Do you believe in miracles, Jared?"

He was silent a long time. "I've never really thought about miracles much," he said honestly, "although they happen every day—medicine, science, babies being born, children growing into adulthood. Those are the kinds of miracles I think about, believe in."

"What do you believe, Jared?" The question slid through my lips as if of its own volition. I needed to know. Of all the things about this man I did and didn't know, this was the most important.

"About what?"

"About God. About Jesus. About faith."

He studied me intently and the silence between us grew. It wasn't an uncomfortable space but a considered one. I felt grateful that I had no desire to fill in the space with nervous chatter.

When he spoke his voice was soft and thoughtful. "Frankly? I spent much of my life as a Revelations 3:15 Christian."

*Revelations 3:15?* He took my surprised silence as a signal to continue. "'I know your works: you are neither hot nor cold. Would it be that you were cold or hot!'"

He shifted in his seat, stretching his long legs and making himself more comfortable. "I spent a lot of my life being lukewarm about Christianity, Sammi. Church was pleasant and familiar, I knew the ropes, the songs, the jargon. I wasn't cold to it, I didn't want it out of my life. In fact, I took comfort in the security of it. I just wasn't 'hot' about it, either. On a scale from one to ten, I hovered between four and six."

He looked at me with a gentle, self-revealing expression that made me feel as though I could read his soul.

"Do you have a gas or electric stove at your house, Sammi?"

Taken aback, I mumbled something about preferring gas to electric.

"Then you know how the pilot light looks in the burner?"

"Of course." Where on earth had this come from? Next, were we going to swap recipes for unleavened bread?

"That was the temperature of my faith—just like the little light in the stove. It was there. It had the potential to start a blazing fire, but was content just 'being there,' lighting up once in a while, but happy to let someone else do the cooking.

"There was a great deal of potential for my faith, but I was content to be barely burning—not hold or cold." He studied me quizzically. "Do you understand what I mean?"

"Perfectly. The church is full of gas ranges with little pilot lights. I don't cook on 'high' in my faith all the time, either."

He looked pleased to know I understood. "The last few years, however, primarily since Molly and I joined forces, someone has been playing with the switches on my stove. I think God gave me Molly to amp up my flame of faith."

He leaned back in his seat and I was struck by his incredible softness and vulnerability. This is what Molly had wanted me to see of her brother. It certainly put me in my little judgmental, holier-than-thou place in a hurry.

"Why do you say that?"

"Because she is such a challenge sometimes." He shook his head as if to rid it of annoying thoughts. "And I see how it is to love people in spite of themselves."

If my heart hadn't already been a puddle resting on my diaphragm, it would have melted then and there.

*What's going on here, God? I don't like this guy, remember? Or at least I didn't last week....*

"But you seemed so angry with her...."

"At her? I suppose so, but I've been angrier with myself. I should have known better than to expect her to change just because she had her name on the front door of the office." He straightened. "But enough about her. I'm sure she didn't get us together to spend our time talking about her."

"Then why *do* you think she tried to link us up?" I teased, knowing the answer already.

He took my right hand and kissed the tip of my index finger. "This."

Gently he moved to my next finger.

"And this."

Okay, my hand is going into paroxysms of joy.

"And this."

By the time he kissed the palm of my hand, I would have followed him like a lemming into the sea. So much for the strong, spirited, independent woman who'd thought Jared would have been best locked out of Molly's home while we were working. He could sort my clutter any old time.

"May I walk you to your room?" he asked.

"It's only up a flight of stairs and down a hall."

"Too far for someone precious like you to travel alone."

We walked hand in hand to the door of my room where we stood facing each other. Jared put his right hand on the door jamb behind me and looked down into my eyes. *Down* into my eyes. I felt small and light and practically waifish.

There were other sensations even more unfamiliar coursing through me, as well. Sensations that played around the words love, captivated, charmed and the scariest word of all, commitment. I felt both relief and sadness when Jared took his hand off the wall behind me and straightened.

"And tomorrow is our last day at the Oasis."

"Back into the desert for us." I felt distressed as I said it.

"How are you getting home?" I was relieved to hear him move to practical issues.

"My camel is in the shop, so Wendy will be picking me up. She went up north. I'll call her to tell her what time to be here."

"Why don't you just ride home with me?"

"Oh, I couldn't…" I began and then stopped myself. I *could.* "I suppose she would like a few more hours with her family. She was disappointed to hear that checkout time here was noon."

"Then call her. Promise her I'll take good care of you, okay?"

I knew he would, and so I did.

## Chapter Twenty-One

I looked back as the Oasis faded into the distance. "I would never in a million years have predicted how this weekend would turn out."

Dreamily I turned to gaze at Jared who, in sunglasses that hid his eyes, a pale blue shirt open at the collar and dark trousers, looked as though he should be driving off a movie set with Julia Roberts instead of me.

He smiled at me and my heart did a flip-flop. *Oh, boy, have I got it bad!*

I may have thought I'd been in love before, but I was mistaken. Anything I'd previously experienced was a pallid version of what I feel right now. That was love. This is *Love*.

Even I, who embraces the safe, secure, organized and planned, can't deny it. There's no doubt in my mind that Jared is the man God has chosen for me. God and I talked about it for most of the last twelve hours and the peace I feel is growing deeper. He is in control. And if God wants this relationship for me, then I want it, too.

Trust Me, God says, and I will work it out.

I glanced at Jared and noticed the muscles of his jaw clenching and unclenching. "Something wrong?"

"I'm eager to apologize to Molly. I got on the Internet and looked up Attention Deficit Disorder. I saw Molly in so many of the descriptions. She has always lived full-out, brave, happy, daring…how she overcomes frustration and still manages to bring so such joy into our family and the lives of others… I think my scattered little sister might be one of my new heroes."

"I'm sure she doesn't hold it against you that you didn't understand, Jared. She couldn't understand it, either, if no one ever diagnosed her."

"No? But she takes responsibility for everything that goes wrong. I gave her too little credit for what has gone *right* for her."

"You're blaming yourself pretty harshly for something we don't even know to be true," I reminded him. "Only a professional can tell you that."

"It doesn't matter. Molly's always looked up to me and expected me to watch out for her. I didn't want to fail her."

My heart went all tender inside. Seeing his humility and the affection he has for his sister makes me even more confident of the wonderful husband and father he will be.

*Husband and father? Whoa! Where'd that come from?*

I am hook, line and sinker in love.

We were nearing the twin cities of Minneapolis and St. Paul when Jared's cell phone rang. I bit back a comment about annoying gadgets being the mosquitoes of the 21$^{st}$ century. I didn't want anything to break the blissful communal silence between us.

Then I tuned in to the sound of Jared's voice on the phone. It was clipped and annoyed? Angry? No, it was *fear*.

"Two hours ago? Why didn't anyone call me right away? Where is she? Don't give me that, Ethan. Of course I'll go directly there. We'll meet you at the hospital and you can take Sammi home."

"Jared?"

He turned to me and his face was ashen. "There's been an accident. Molly…"

I recalled the trip she'd been planning with her friends.

"Lost control…had seat belt on…saved her life…unconscious…neurological emergency…haven't been able to wake her…my parents are there…"

The disjointed words came through my stunned fog. "But will she be all right?"

The look in his eyes terrified me. "Ethan says they don't know yet. Once she wakes up…if she does…" He cleared his throat. "Ethan says there's no wound on her head but a large bruise…."

I couldn't speak, not that it would have mattered. There were no words that could comfort Jared at this moment.

"Jared, slow down. The last thing your family needs is another accident." I don't mind speed, being a downhill skier and all, but I don't like buildings blurring past me on city streets.

He took his foot off the accelerator and let the car slow into the vague vicinity of the speed limit, but his hands remained clutched, white-knuckled, on the wheel.

"Call Ethan again, will you?" he ordered. "See if anything has changed."

Reluctantly I picked up the phone and dialed.

"Ethan here."

"Hi, it's Sammi. Any—"

"No change. She's stable, the bones she's broken are set, and except for the huge bruise on her head, she looks pretty good. One of the others in the car has gone into surgery for internal bleeding but everyone is optimistic. The doctors won't say much about the fact that Molly is unconscious.

There is edema in the brain, and it takes time for the swelling to subside. The edema is causing intracranial pressure, which is contributing to her unconsciousness. They aren't willing to give a prognosis quite yet. They say it could be a while." His voice wavered. "How is Jared—really?"

"As you'd expect," I said, trying to keep from analyzing Jared in his presence.

"Is he feeling guilty?" Ethan asked unexpectedly.

"Why do you ask?"

"Because I know him. He's running the tape of his life backward trying to think of every time he might have disappointed Molly and is beating himself up over it. He's also wondering how he could have prevented this, never taking into account that Molly's a grown woman and makes her own decisions. Jared has compassion and understanding for everyone but himself. He is the only one he expects to be perfect."

"A hard task," I murmured softly, but Jared heard me.

"What's 'hard'? Something with Molly? Let me talk to him." He swiped for the phone and I pulled it away.

"Don't mix driving and cell-phone conversations. And we weren't talking about Molly, we were talking about you." I returned to the phone. "I have to go, Ethan. We'll be there in less than twenty minutes."

I ended the call and turned to Jared. "Nothing has changed. I don't think we'll have any answers until the swelling within the skull goes down. For right now, all we can do is pray."

After what seemed like forever, we pulled up at the hospital. I was out the car door almost before it stopped and Jared was close behind me.

A wave of hospital scent assaulted my nose as we entered. No matter what products the cleaning crews use, they can't take away the distinctive smell of disinfectants, rubbing alcohol and the harsh chemical odor of industrial cleaning products. Even a cleaning nut like me dislikes it.

"Where is Molly Hamilton?" Jared asked the woman at the front desk.

We were directed through a maze of halls that spewed us out into a huge circular room with quick-moving nurses and a hub of machines discharging readouts. Intensive care. Ethan appeared out of a small waiting room and grabbed Jared by the shoulders.

He led us into a darkened, windowless room with straight-backed chairs ringing the walls. There were two lamps on small tables and an assortment of unappealing magazines. A TV flickered in the dimness. Wrestling was on. Someone was trying to leap off the ropes and smash an opponent into oblivion. Great viewing choice for an intensive care unit.

Then I noticed an older couple rising. The gentleman was tall and stately with gray hair and small, well-groomed mustache. He was dressed in what my mother called "church clothes," a suit and tie, well-polished wing tips and, to prove my mother right, a church bulletin folded in half and sticking out of one pocket. The woman beside him was slender and just as dignified looking. She, too, wore church clothes—a navy suit, white blouse and extraordinarily expensive-looking pearls. Her white hair was cut short and swept back like wings from her pretty face. A face that looked just like Molly's.

Jared first embraced his mother and then his father.

"How is she?"

"The same. They'll be releasing her to a room soon." The older man's voice held much the same timbre as Jared's.

"Shouldn't they keep her here in ICU where she can be watched more closely?"

"Apparently they don't feel the need. They can monitor her state of consciousness from her room."

Jared opened his mouth to speak and then remembered that he had me in tow.

"Mom, Dad, I'm sorry. I should introduce you. This is Sammi Smith, my..."

Whatever he was going to call me was left unsaid because his mother, Geneva, came at me with open arms.

"Molly has told me so much about you! She adores you, Ms. Smith. Why, I was at her place the other day and there was counter space, empty chairs and such an amazing difference in her attitude. You're a miracle worker!"

*Don't I wish. I'd have Molly standing on her feet right now.*

"Thank you. I love her, too. She's a remarkable woman."

Jared's father, Robert Hamilton, stepped forward. "It's time we met. I'm just sorry it's under these circumstances."

*Even now, they're thinking about me.* There didn't seem to be a selfish bone running through any of Jared's family.

"I'm so sorry about this. Is there anything you can...tell us?"

"Not much. Molly's friend was driving. They hadn't gotten far out of the Cities."

"I suppose they were hurrying," Geneva picked up the story. "It's just like Molly and her friends to do that."

"Apparently the driver lost control of the car. That's all we know."

"Can I see her?" Jared asked softly. I could feel the tension he was attempting to harness in his body.

"Yes. Room 545, on the other side of the nurses' station. Just tell someone you're going in."

Jared started for the door, then paused. "Sammi, would you like to come with me?"

I took his hand.

"Jared, is there anything I can do?"

"Just be here, Sammi. I can't string two clear thoughts together in my head right now."

I opened my mouth to give him reassurances and closed it again. Anything I might have said would be palliative words with no corroboration. Jared deserved more than that.

Together we walked through a tangled maze of machines and wires into the cubicle where Molly lay.

# *Chapter Twenty-Two*

Monitors were humming and lights blinking on various machines, but the centerpiece of the room was unmoving. I had to look twice to make sure the sheet over Molly's chest was rising and falling rhythmically with her breath.

She appeared to be sleeping. But for a nasty bruise that stained the side of her face and forehead, she might have been dozing on her own couch.

Jared flinched and I felt palpable waves of dismay emanating from him. He was in more pain than Molly. Cautiously he moved forward, bent over the bed and placed his hand over her still one.

"Molly? Hey, it's Jared. How are you doing, honey?"

His tone was so gentle that I felt my heart shattering.

"Sammi and I just got back from the Oasis. It was great, sweetie, really great. You'd better pull yourself together so I can take you and Sammi back there, okay?"

He pulled a chair up to her bedside and sat down. I took another and joined him. We sat there for what seemed like hours, Jared talking to Molly as if she heard and understood his every word. He told her stories about the spa, the food, the romance party and how we'd driven home together this morning. Remarkably, his voice was conversational, even, calm.

His face, however, belied his tone. His forehead was furrowed and a deep crease slashed itself between his eyebrows. The brackets around his mouth had grown deeply carved just since we had arrived. Still, he held Molly's hand and spoke to her gently.

Geneva Hamilton entered, put her hand on her son's shoulder and murmured, "I'd like to spend time with Molly, Jared. Why don't you and Sammi visit with Ethan for a while?"

He nodded, gave his sister's hand a squeeze and rose.

Outside the room he said, "I've read that sometimes people in that state can actually hear what's going on around them. I don't want anyone in there talking 'about' her and not 'to' her. What if she can hear? She would be so frightened…."

His family seemed in complete agreement without ever having discussed that strategy. I could hear Geneva telling Molly about the gardens at home. Then she began to unwind a long tale about the state of her tomatoes. She sounded as though Molly were sitting across from her listening intently.

Ethan met us outside the door to the family lounge. "Your parents haven't eaten. They were just leaving church when they got the word…." Ethan bit his lip. "Do you want to take them downstairs for lunch?"

"I need to stay here. I want to talk to the doctor." Jared's voice was brusque and businesslike. "You and Sammi can take them."

"I'll stay here with you," I offered.

"You haven't eaten, either. Besides, my mother will like getting to know you." He gave me a shadow of a smile. "It's fine. I'm okay."

*Fine? Hah!* But there was no arguing with him. Ethan shepherded us down to the nearly empty lunchroom in the bowels of the hospital.

Geneva sank into the chair Robert pulled out for her and gave a weary sigh.

"What can we do for you, Geneva?" Ethan asked. "For any of you?"

"It would be nice if you could keep my son's head screwed on straight," Robert Hamilton stated bluntly.

"Excuse me…" I began, but Ethan seemed to know exactly what the older man meant.

"He's afraid Jared will get completely wrapped up in Molly's situation to the exclusion of everything else." Ethan looked at Geneva. "What is it you call the two of them?"

"Identical twins born eight and a half years and a gender apart," she supplied. "Those two watched out for and protected each other as though they were joined at the hip. It's quite remarkable, really, considering the age difference between them, but they've always been close." Geneva's eyes grew troubled. "It's bad enough to have Molly in such a state. We don't want to have to worry about Jared, too."

"Worry about him?" I echoed.

The elder Hamilton took my hand. "How long have you known Jared, my dear?"

*Long enough to fall in love with him.*

"A few weeks."

"Then there is still much you have to discover about my son—all of it good. One of the best and most difficult things about him is his capacity for love. It takes Jared a long time to give his heart to someone, but then there's no getting it back."

"We're afraid," Geneva continued, "that he'll let go of everything and put all his energy into Molly's situation." She glanced timidly at her husband. "And the doctor said he had no idea how long it might be until Molly awakens. According to him, there are many levels of unconsciousness, from coma to obtundation and lethargy. A patient's progress is measured by an increasing awareness of stimuli. When Molly begins to emerge, she'll begin to respond to stimuli."

*And what if she doesn't?*

The horrible thought stung me. I thought of Jared bent over Molly's bed. Suddenly the sweet normalcy and fragile regularity of our lives were tied to that one small frame in that large hospital bed.

*Lord, what's this about? Help this family! Put Your tender, protective, healing hand on Molly. And show me my place in all of this. Father, how can I be Your light and love for these people in this troubled time?*

The atmosphere seemed to lighten as we ate and I was struck by what strong, gracious people the Hamiltons are. As soon as Molly improved, things would return to normal…*normal.* I closed my eyes and sighed.

"What is it?" Ethan asked.

"I just thought of something Jared and I were discussing before we heard about the accident, something about Molly. In passing, I mentioned that some of Molly's short attention span and difficulty getting organized might be attributable to Attention Deficit Disorder. Jared, of course, began researching it on the computer this morning. He was concerned because Molly has so many of the symptoms of the disorder. If that were the case, he believes he would have handled their partnership differently, giving Molly more support in the areas she needed it. I hate to say it, but Jared was already feeling guilty over his sister before this happened."

Ethan groaned but it was Geneva who spoke. "Jared's standards for himself are higher than he holds for any other living being."

"It's why he's so successful and so driven," Robert added.

"And so unforgiving of himself," Geneva concluded.

"I can just about hear what he's thinking right now," Ethan

said. "'If only I'd done this…or that…or paid more attention to what was going on with Molly….'"

In other words, what I loved about him might just be his downfall.

# Chapter Twenty-Three

"Hi, this is Jared. I'm unable to take your call right now. Please leave your number and I'll return your call as soon as I can."

I hung up my phone without leaving a message.

"Still not picking up?" Wendy asked. She was snapping fresh beans into a big colander for tonight's dinner.

"He can't have it on when he's in the hospital."

"And he's always at the hospital."

I didn't respond. Anything I'd say would only sound selfish. I don't begrudge a minute of the time Jared spends with Molly, but I am getting a little frightened. He's not been himself. Even Ethan says so.

"What is it, Sammi? What are you *not* saying?"

I considered saying nothing, but Wendy knows me too well. I might as well spill it now as have her nagging me until she gets it out of me, anyway. "He's withdrawing from me. I can feel him shrinking away, not just from me but from everyone. He works twelve hours a day, sits at the hospital for seven and sleeps for five. If Ethan and I didn't go to the hospital, we'd never see him."

"There's more to it than that," Wendy said astutely.

I nodded unhappily. "He's blaming himself for everything but the high price of oil and the fact that mosquitoes bite. He and Molly have a bond that he thinks he broke by losing his cool with her. And—" I couldn't suppress the crackle of emotion in my voice "—the longer she remains unconscious, the more he's afraid…"

"That she won't wake up?" Leave it to Wendy to tell it like it is.

"It's been five days since the accident." I grabbed a handful of beans and started snapping them. If felt good, a way to vent my frustration on something productive. Snap, snap, snap.

"Hey! I thought this was my job. You're supposed to be peeling potatoes."

Wendy has been a trouper, coming to my place every evening with a bag of groceries and a new recipe to try for dinner. It's a helpful distraction and I like to cook, but if this routine goes on much longer, I'm going to look like a very tall, very round pumpkin.

"The other thing," I said hesitantly, not quite sure how to put it in to words, "he's become very silent about God."

Wendy peeked at the water on the stove to see if it was boiling.

"I…I have a feeling Jared isn't putting his full trust onto God right now."

"Seems like this would be a *great* time to be talking to the Big Guy." Wendy plopped the potatoes I'd peeled into the roiling water.

"Jared's still withdrawing."

Wendy put dishes on the eating counter and shooed Zelda off one of the stools. "Scram. Go flash your rhinestones somewhere else."

Zelda, as if she'd understood, stood up, gave Wendy a dirty look and moved herself to the window seat, where the light hit her just right and her collar sent prisms of color all over the room.

"Drama queen," Wendy muttered under her breath.

"You're just jealous because you don't have jewelry as nice as Zelda's." I checked the roast in the oven. It would be done at the same time as the potatoes. At least was one small victory. I clock my meals to the minute so that everything is done at exactly the same time. Ben says he likes me because I'm even more reliable than The Timer. He's coming to dinner, too, so I wanted to have things progressing like clockwork.

"Why don't you buy *me* some nice jewelry?" Wendy groused. "You buy all hers."

"Okay, next time I go to Norah's Ark, come with me. We'll pick out something pretty."

"I didn't mean at the pet shop."

I smiled sweetly at her. "I did."

The banter didn't dissuade me from our more serious conversation. "Do you remember Mike Simmons?" I asked. Mike was a fellow Wendy had dated in college.

"Of course I do. He made the best fried green tomatoes and deep fried French toast I've ever had. Of course, if he didn't have a vat of grease to cook his food in he was helpless. Why do you ask?"

"Remember talking with Mike about God, Jesus, forgiveness and salvation?"

"Like talking to a brick wall," Wendy recalled. "A head hard as stone."

"But that wasn't it, was it?"

Wendy paused as she was running cold water over the beans to wash them.

"No. It really wasn't. But it took a long time for me to figure out what was going on with him."

She turned off the water, set the beans in the sink to drip, wiped her hands on a dishtowel and sat down on the stool Zelda had vacated. "Mike was the first person I'd ever run into who admitted to me that he thought he wasn't 'good enough' for God. He thought he'd done too much, been too 'bad' to face God with it.

"'I've done too much bad stuff,' he told me. 'God won't have anything to do with me. There's no way He'd forgive me for the things I've done.'" Wendy sat back and crossed her arms. "Wow. I'd forgotten about that. Poor Mike really suffered over that notion. It took a long time to convince him otherwise." She turned to me. "You remember, you were there."

I did remember, vividly. That's why I'd brought up his name. Mike had come from a dysfunctional home. He'd practically raised himself and had made some bad choices—drugs, a gang, even criminal activity. He was an angry young man. So angry that when his father died, he refused to attend the funeral.

"God's not going to forgive me for that," he once told me. "No way, no how. And nothing you can tell me is going to make me believe that He is."

We'd sat with that, stuck in the mud, for weeks, months. Mike, sure that God wasn't big enough to forgive him, didn't realize that the real problem was that Mike refused to forgive himself.

"Are you saying that you think Jared is in the same place Mike was?"

"Maybe I am." And I told Wendy the entire story of Molly's mistakes, Jared's anger with her, Molly's plea for him to fire her. Then I told her about Jared's research on ADD. Knowing that ADD might be partly responsible for Molly's trouble had made everything happening now seem, if possible, even worse.

"And what does he think he could have done about it?"

"I'm not sure. He says he should have given her more structure and direction, that he should have been more compassionate and recognized what was going on with her."

"Before or after he walked on water?" Wendy asked,

rolling her eyes. "The guy's not omnipotent. Why is he giving himself such a hard time?"

Before I could say more, the doorbell rang and Imelda leaped off the couch where she'd been camping, woofing wildly. She ran for the door, skidded on the hardwood floor until her nails—brilliant orange, the polish bottle said "sun-kissed"—hooked on a throw rug and sent her sliding sideways to the door, barking liken a banshee. Just as Ben threw open the door, Imelda's body hit him in the shins and sent him sailing back out into the hall.

I closed my eyes at the sound of the crash and ensuing silence. Then Ben roared, "Get off my chest and quit licking my face!"

He staggered into the kitchen carrying a small sack and looking like he'd just tangled with an octopus. "Here. For you. Later. When you need it."

I peered into the bag. Godiva chocolate ice cream. For medicinal purposes only. And the heel of a man's shoe for Imelda.

"Are you all right?" I asked. Wendy was too busy grinning to be a decent hostess.

"Other than my pride, my tibia, fibula and sacrum, yes. Why don't you let someone besides Imelda answer the door? Like Wendy?"

"Because I can't bark as loud or slide as well," Wendy said cheerfully, and held out a plate of cheese, crackers and sliced veggies. "Appetizer?"

After dinner, we retreated to my living room with hot coffee and a plate of, what else? Chocolates.

"That was great, you guys," Ben said appreciatively as he patted his concave stomach. "Now I won't have to cook for three more days."

"What? Is The Timer nonoperational?"

"It is, but I've been working on something really cool. Magic tricks."

"Tricks?" I said. Imelda looked up from her place on the hearth rug.

"Yeah. Want to see one?" Ben stood up and with a flourish, pulled a white hankie out of his pocket, then a blue one tied on the tail of the white, then a red, an orange, a purple, a green…until there was a bolt of hankie fabric strewn across the floor. Then, as Ben's flourishes and showmanship gained speed, he pulled his pocket inside out and loose change skittered across the floor, too.

"Oops. That wasn't supposed to happen."

"Aren't you supposed to pull that stuff out of a hat or something?"

"You probably wouldn't have let me in the house if I'd come wearing a top hat," Ben pointed out sensibly.

"Imelda might have. She isn't all that discerning in areas other than shoes."

"Besides, I'm just practicing. Want to see a quarter come out of your ear?"

"How can I see it if it's coming out of *my* ear?"

"Wendy will watch and vouch for it." Ben picked a quarter off the floor, fumbled a bit behind my ear and announced, "Ta-dah!"

"Yep, that was her ear, all right," Wendy said. "What'd you do, order a kit from the back of a comic book?"

Ben sat down heavily, as if the tricks had exhausted him. "I decided I need a hobby, and everything else is too messy or takes too much time. I'm already messy enough and have too little time. I can practice this whenever I want. When I get better, I think I'll add some pyrotechnics…."

*One more thing to add to my prayer list.*

It was after ten o'clock when Wendy said, "I'd better get going. How does salmon and dilled potatoes sound for tomorrow?"

"Great. Want me to get the groceries?"

"Sure, if you're going out," Wendy said as she disappeared in the direction of her car.

"What's that about?" Ben asked, always interested when food is concerned.

"She's made me her mission. She comes over every night and we cook dinner together. It's really nice, if I do say so myself. It keeps me busy and leaves less time on my hands in the evening."

"Your friend isn't any better, then?"

"No. And the rest of the family seems to be getting worse." I filled him in on what Wendy and I had been discussing.

"And Jared doesn't think his sister should be left alone?"

"He's hoping that if he keeps talking to her, he'll somehow pull her back, out of this unconscious state. He doesn't want anyone to speak harshly around her or say anything that might upset her on the off chance that…"

"I get it. Maybe I could come to the hospital someday and visit with Molly so you could talk to Jared."

"Ben, that is so sweet, but you don't even know Molly…." Suddenly I felt very silly. "Of course, she *is* unconscious."

"I'm told I have a pleasant voice. I'll tell her about my research. It will be a thrill a minute for her." He grinned and planted a kiss on my forehead.

"You are a friend in need and a friend indeed. Thanks. I might take you up on it. I would like to spend some time with Jared."

"Great, let me know when we're going. Oh, and by the way," he said, giving me a big grin, "I *really* like salmon and dilled potatoes."

## *Chapter Twenty-Four*

If I invent plastic produce bags that comes off a roll in the grocery store and open on the first try, I'll save shoppers hours of time and frustration. And, if I ever figure out how dead bugs get into enclosed light fixtures, I'll revolutionize the lighting industry.

These are the profound thoughts I have while working with clients. I rarely voice them for fear that they will have me (a) evaluated by a trained therapist or (b) locked away.

Of course, sometimes clients contribute to the insanity-making, too.

Enter the Julia Child of household bedlam and anarchy, my client Bonnie and her three sons, who can cook up calamity like others cook up pasta.

"Little Roy has been studying the concept of volume in school. You know, like how many gallons of water there are in the ocean. Whoever would have thought that he'd try to figure out the volume of water in his waterbed?" Bonnie looked at me with a mix of delight, pride and dismay. "Do you think it will ever dry out down here?"

I took out the notebook I carry, looked up a phone number,

jotted it down on a slip of paper and handed it to Bonnie, whose real last name is Cochran. "This is the name and number of a fabulous carpet cleaner. He will come in and do whatever is necessary. I'd recommend you call him. It's going to get musty in here very soon."

"Oh, thank you!" She tucked the paper into the pocket of her Hilfigers. "Little Roy has allergies. We can't let that happen."

I considered pointing out that the moldy birds' nests, decaying fauna, decomposing skeleton of something that may once have been a reptile and the stale food rotting in plates around Little Roy's room were probably having an equally grave effect on the child. Of course, they were no doubt science projects of one sort or another and hence, cute and clever, like the queen-sized water bed, its contents now spread across a good portion of the lower level of their house.

"Maybe we should go upstairs," Bonnie suggested. "I have some other things to consult you about."

*Oh, yeah. Uh-huh. I'll bet you do.*

I'd seen her three hoodlum sons grinding Cheetos into her ivory carpet when I came in.

Dutifully I followed her into "Big Ronnie's" room. Ronnie, it appeared, was the oldest of the boys, but named more for his size than his rank in the family pecking order.

"He was experimenting with some household products. He wants to be an inventor when he grows up." She stared at the ragged hole in the carpet, the polka dotted white patches in the bedspread and then up at the smoke stain on the ceiling. "I guess I shouldn't have let him use the bleach. I had no idea it could be combustible."

Then she looked up hopefully. "Someday I know we'll be so proud of our boys and what they accomplish."

*If they don't blow up the house first.*

I wrote down a few more numbers—interior painters,

reliable one-day carpet installers and places I know that sell high-quality bedspreads…cheap.

"And, of course, there's Middy's room."

"'Middy'? As in 'middle'?" *Say it isn't so!*

She looked at me, shocked. "Whatever made you think that? Middy is short for Roy Middleton Cochran junior. He's named after his father."

*Of course. Why didn't I think of that?*

It also explained "Little Roy."

"What's been going on in Middy's room?" I asked

"Frankly I'd be more upset if I he'd done it on a whim, but he really does want to be a physicist when he grows up."

"Yes, and…" *Didn't physicists put together the atom bomb?*

"I'm not sure if this was supposed to be an experiment in centrifugal force or gravitational pull, but…"

A small darting missile in a red T-shirt and a baseball cap bolted by and Bonnie, with a swiftness that impressed me, reached out and stopped its trajectory. "Middy, will you explain to Ms. Smith what you were doing in your bedroom when…you know."

Middy looked at me with an expression that said he would die from terminal boredom if he had to have an entire conversation with me, but he did open his mouth, and gobbledygook spewed out.

"Centrifugal force doesn't really exist, but an object traveling in a circle will behave as if it is experiencing some outward force. This is the force we call centrifugal force. This 'force' depends on the mass of the object, the speed of the rotation and how far the object is from the center. The bigger the object, the greater the speed in which it is traveling and the more distance the object is from the center, the greater the force.

"It's like being on a merry-go-round. It's harder for Mom or Dad to stay on it without exerting some inward force because their masses are greater." Middy got an evil look in his eye. "Dad's fat."

"Now, Middy," Bonnie said placidly. "He's big-boned."

"Whatever." And he bolted off.

"He's explained it to me before, but the boys are so *bright* I barely understand them sometimes."

I took a breath, opened the door to Middy's room and entered what felt like a Jackson Pollock abstract splatter painting. Red paint was splashed on every white wall in a rather intriguing-looking asymmetrical pattern of loops and splatters. There was also a huge red splash mark in the center of the beige carpet and above, a ceiling fan hanging by its wires and a bit of Sheetrock.

"Middy likes it this way and wants me to leave it, but I just don't know," Bonnie said. "It will be very hard to decorate around."

"What is 'it'?" I was in total awe of the disarray. This made my short list of all-time worst messes. It was as amazing as one of the wonders of the world—the Taj Mahal of paint damage.

"Middy had been to the doctor for his checkup. They did a blood test and he, of course, demanded to know what they were going to do with it. The technician explained how it's spun out and tested. Middy was fascinated by the concept of centrifugal force so he decided to see how spinning a can of paint might work. Naturally, he thought of using his ceiling fan to do the spinning."

*Oh, naturally.*

"Bonnie, I've given you the names of the people you need to contact, the painter, carpet people and oh, yes, I'll give you the name of an electrician in this area who is very good. But I don't think you need *me*. I'm a personal organizer and clutter coach. This…your boys…are out of my area of expertise."

I was trying to recall a good child therapist I could recommend when Bonnie said, "Maybe you're right. It didn't occur to me until just now that all the boys really need is a little direction in their areas of interest. An art tutor, perhaps, or someone in the sciences...." She clapped her hands together delightedly. "Thank you, Sammi. You have helped me a lot whether you know it or not."

"Delighted to be of service."

I hot-footed it down the steps and to my car as Mrs. Cochran stood in the door waving. I didn't want to be around when she turned to go into the house and saw what was going on behind her back.

I think Middy was preparing to test a theory of how fast Little Roy would slide down a banister with rocks in his pockets.

Ben arrived at my house carrying a plastic grocery sack. He was dressed in high-water jeans, a shirt buttoned to the top button on the collar and festooned with pen protectors, and tennis shoes—Keds.

"Do you have a Geeks Anonymous meeting today?" I asked when I opened the door.

He looked down at himself as if just registering what he was wearing. Then he shrugged. Fortunately for Ben, he would have been handsome dressed in a diaper and masquerading as Baby New Year.

"This will do. I was wondering if I could come to the hospital with you today. I'd like to see Molly."

"Absolutely. I appreciate it." Jared grows more and more morose each day that Molly doesn't respond. Frankly, Geneva is almost as worried about him as she is about Molly.

"He was this way as a child," she'd told me. "Tough as nails except where it came to Molly. The only times I ever saw him cry was when Molly got hurt. He'd stoically let me wash his cuts and scraps, but let Molly fall off her bike…." Geneva had shaken her head. "Then they'd both be worked up."

She'd paused and gotten a faraway look in her eyes. "I know why he was so protective, but I could never figure out how to temper it in him."

My face must have shown my confusion because she had smiled.

"My father was still living when Molly was born. He was ill, but hanging on by sheer willpower to see his new grand-daughter. It meant so much to him." Geneva had sighed then. "Anyway, I caught them together one day—my father and Jared in Molly's bedroom. She was sound asleep in her crib. Jared was looking through the bars of the crib and Father was watching both of them."

She was silent for a long time before she had continued. "I'll never forget what my father said to Jared. I wish I'd spoken up back then, but I had no idea of the impact on him at the time or how he took it to heart. He said, 'Jared, from now on, Molly is your responsibility. Take care of her for me, will you?'

"It reminded me of what Jesus said to John from the cross. It's in John 19, verses 26 and 27. '*When Jesus saw his mother and the disciple whom he loved standing beside her, he said to his mother, "Woman, here is your son." Then he said to the disciple, "Here is your mother." And from that hour the disciple took her into his home.*'

"It was only weeks later that my father died. I recalled it later and realized that it felt in that moment that my father, Jared's grandfather, had commissioned Jared to care for Molly, that he was specially made for the job and no one else could do it better. He took his grandfather's death very hard. He was only eight years old, after all, and the relationship between him and Molly was set." *Commissioned.* That's significant in the Bible. In Numbers, the Lord said to Moses,

"Take Joshua…and lay your hand on him, have him stand before Eleazar the priest and all the congregation, and commission him in their sight." In Deuteronomy when the Lord commissioned Joshua, He said, "Be strong and bold, for you shall bring the Israelites into the land that I promised them. I will be with you." Being appointed by God is a huge deal, no matter how one looks at it.

Gradually I was beginning to understand Jared's dedication to Molly. What would I have thought at eight years old if I'd been given such a responsibility by someone I loved deeply? I remembered my own grandfather's booming voice and large stature. Sometimes I childishly assumed he was God's spokesperson. Since he was a pastor and an imposing presence, it only made sense. Why wouldn't a young Jared see his own grandfather in much the same way?

And then, after appointing him Molly's guardian, Jared's grandfather died and the commission was sealed.

"I'm sure by now Jared would dismiss that episode as a mere childhood incident, but I know how deeply it affected him at the time…and has ever since. Consciously or unconsciously, Molly has been 'his' ever since she was born."

Geneva had smiled wanly and my heart went out to her. "Until recently, neither my husband nor I have thought it a bad thing. Molly's been a handful sometimes, and we've needed Jared in the mix."

"What was she like as a child in school?"

"Oh, my, she was a note a week from the teacher! 'Smart,' they'd say, but a 'discipline problem' or 'has a poor attention span' or 'cannot quit talking in class.' Every teacher loved her sunny personality and loving disposition and yet they all tore their hair out over her." Geneva had paused before adding, "Not much different than the present day."

Tears had welled in her eyes and spilled onto her cheeks. "Sammi, I'm so worried about both of them."

Both Molly and Jared were slipping away. Not only was Molly's well-being in grave jeopardy, but so was any "happily ever after" Jared and I had been anticipating.

## Chapter Twenty-Five

Ben's been acting very peculiar. It's difficult to tell when Ben's being odd and when he's just being Ben, but something is up. I stopped at his place to compare the framed photo Aunt Gertie had sent me with the one she'd sent to him.

Aunt Gertie frightens me sometimes. Ever since her contemporary "mood" started, she's been sending us strange and wonderful surrealistic photography. It's always beautifully mounted and for a while I thought that she was buying it at some wigged out art gallery she'd found. Recently, however, Ben told me that it is my aunt who is taking the pictures and her husband Arthur doing the framing.

It's been entertaining trying to guess what her subject matter is, because she zeros in on one point in an object and photographs it in great detail—like the pocket on a pair of Levi's jeans, a pomegranate, the bottom of the trash can and once, horribly, Arthur flexing a muscle. I was never sure *which* muscle, exactly, and didn't dare ask.

The latest offering is the weirdest yet. I have several guesses as to what it might be, but I want to consult with Ben, who usually "gets" Aunt Gertie before I do.

I knocked and walked into his house with my gift in hand. On the table in the foyer was the other half of my set, a photograph of…well…it could have been a close-up of a very tiny Rorschach test, an outbreak of black measles, something Gertie had grown in a Petri dish or age spots on an elderly hand.

"What do you think?" Ben walked into the foyer with a bowl of cereal in one hand and a spoon in the other.

I offered my guesses. He shook his head at each one.

"Nope. At first I thought it was a close-up of the back of old, mildewed wallpaper—the wicked looking decomposing spots and all—but I finally got it."

"What is it?" I refuse to hang anything on my walls that might be in questionable taste—especially Arthur's bicep or oblique.

"I've got one going in the kitchen." Ben waved his spoon in that direction.

I followed him into the room which looked much like it always did—a mad scientist's laboratory. There's never much actual food in Ben's kitchen but you can take your pick of weird strains of who-knows-what in his fridge. Actually, today there was more food than usual; a loaf of bread, a carton of orange juice and a bowl of moldy fruit.

I edged nearer the fruit and squinted. Something was coming into view. I glanced at my photo and back at the fruit. "It's rotting bananas!" I crowed.

"Bingo. That banana she photographed has some age on it, that's for sure. That Gertie, she's something, isn't she?"

Something, yes. What, I'm not sure.

"Are you going to the hospital?" Ben asked.

"Yes. I don't have another client this afternoon so I thought I'd stop by." *And see Jared.*

"Can I come with you? I made something for Molly." He held up a device that looked like a portable headset with a flashlight hooked to it by a long piece of stiff wire. "Music, light and color all at once. Or books on tapes." He looked up hopefully. "It might work."

I sank onto a chair but resisted the urge to bury my head in my hands. "The doctors are puzzled as to why she hasn't come out of this yet. She reacts negatively to loud noises, for example, and positively to her family's voices. The longer this goes on…"

My time with Jared at the Oasis seemed like it was a million years ago.

It had occurred to me—sometime in the night when Imelda and Zelda were jockeying for position in my bed and woke me—that if Molly didn't wake up and Jared continued to blame himself for not saving Molly from herself, there was no future for Jared and me, either.

"He has no mercy for himself, Ben. He won't forgive himself for firing her, for losing it over the damage she did to the company."

"I thought he was a Christian," Ben said bluntly. "That he knew God forgives him."

"But he doesn't forgive himself."

"So he thinks his word counts for more than God's?"

My head snapped up.

"If Jared won't accept God's forgiveness because he can't forgive himself, then he thinks his problems are too big for God, that he knows better than God, right?"

Wendy's friend Mike had learned that lesson. Just as we'd had to turn Molly over to God's healing hand, Jared had to surrender his guilt and regret to God, as well. As long as he held on to it, he was flying in the face of God's promise to forgive and wipe our sins away. While Molly was in a physical crisis, Jared was in a crisis of *trust*.

"Come on, Ben, let's go. I want to talk to Jared."

Ben gathered up his invention for Molly and followed me

toward the door. On impulse, I picked up my photo of Aunt Gertie's rotting banana and took it with me.

Jared looked up as Ben and I entered the room.

He'd lost weight. His belt was a notch tighter and his tailored white shirt seemed loose around the collar beneath his tie. He was also taking on the pallor of the hospital lights as his energy drained out the soles of his feet.

Molly, on the other hand, looked wonderful. Geneva made sure her hair was always fixed and had even given her daughter a manicure. Mrs. Hamilton said that Molly would be furious if she woke up and realized she looked a mess.

"Hey," Jared said as he lifted a hand in greeting. "Thanks for coming."

I walked over and kissed Molly on the cheek. "It's me. Sammi. I brought something for you to look at." I propped the photo of the rotting banana skin on the bed table. "I'll bet you can't figure out what it is. Of course, you'll have to open your eyes to see it."

Then I heard a paroxysm of throat clearing. "And I brought you a playmate. Ben is here."

I suppose it was wishful thinking, but I would have sworn that one corner of her lip tipped in a smile.

Ben loped over to the bed and whipped his new contraption out of his pocket. "I made this for you, Molly. I think you're going to like it. And I have the most amazing magic tricks to show you…."

Jared and I escaped into the hallway.

"Thanks for bringing Ben," he said as he wearily rubbed his neck. "I can't say why, but I feel like Molly must enjoy him—or she would, if she could."

"Then she's in good hands. Want to take a walk?"

We headed for a small park on the hospital grounds with a few scattered picnic tables, grills and a cover of trees.

Jared rolled his shoulders as we walked. "Feels good to move. I've been frozen over Molly's bed. I suppose I think if I sit there, willing her to wake up, she'll do it."

"And what does the doctor say?"

"That the swelling in her head is going down slowly. That now would be a wonderful time for Molly to open her eyes."

I leaned back against a big oak tree, savoring the feel of something solid and real against my body. Nothing else about trips to the hospital ever felt real anymore. We were all living in a surrealistic dream from which we wanted to wake.

Jared put his palms against the oak over my head and looked down at me. Then he leaned down and kissed my forehead so gently it felt as though a butterfly had landed there.

"You've been awfully faithful, coming here every day, keeping our spirits up. Mom and Dad think you're the best thing since, as Dad says, 'sliced bread.'"

"Your parents are amazing. I know now why you and Molly are so wonderful."

"But it's taking a toll on them. They aren't young. I wish they would stay home and get more rest. I've told them that I'll be here for Molly."

"What about work? You have to go to the office."

"I can work on my laptop in Molly's room."

"Jared," I ventured, feeling my way gingerly along this slippery slope, "what if…"

His eyes emptied of life.

"We have to face it, Jared. Molly may not come back to us."

"Sammi, there's something I want to talk to you about." His voice sounded hollow to my ears. "I don't want you to be saddled with this. You didn't buy into this scenario when we were…you know, back at the Oasis. You don't have to stay…."

"Is there something wrong with *your* head, too? What are you talking about?"

"Sammi, I love you. But it's becoming clearer and clearer that it might be more loving to let you live without me and this enormous responsibility…."

"Get a grip, Jared. I'm not running away from this."

"I know. You wouldn't do that. You'd stick with us because you are considerate, caring, courageous and strong…."

"You're describing a Girl Scout, Jared, not a woman in love. I *want* to be here—for you, for Molly, for your parents. I *want* it."

"I can't let you…."

"You can't stop me, either."

Jared scraped his fingers through his hair in frustration. "It would be so much better for you if…"

"If you quit talking nonsense." Then I remembered the conversation I'd had with Ben. "Jared, you just don't *trust*. You don't trust me, you don't trust God…."

"What do you mean, I don't trust God?"

"You think that God can't forgive you…or won't…." I struggled for what I wanted to say. "No, that's not it. You think that God *shouldn't* forgive you! You don't trust Him to be God. You're making Him small by filtering Him through your finite understanding. Don't you see?"

I wondered if he even heard me. He was so far into his own thoughts that I was probably like a noisy chickadee, chattering background noise in this depth of despondency.

"Thank you, Sammi, but we can't ignore this."

"No. But we can get through it. Together. Us. You, me. *Together.*"

I was having about as much effect as a ping-pong ball bouncing against a skyscraper—none.

He took me by the elbow and steered me back toward the hospital. "We'll talk about this again, Sammi. When you aren't so emotional."

*Me? Emotional? It takes one to know one!*

As we walked together, Jared's hand firmly on my arm, I began to realize that, if Jared thought he was protecting me by pulling out of my life, he would do it.

I have to get it through his loveable, altruistic, thickheaded skull that the only way to protect me was to bring me closer, not to push me away.

# Chapter Twenty-Six

It was a relief to have multiple appointments today. That kept me from obsessing too much about what I was going to do about Jared and his insistence that I would be better off without him.

First of all, stubborn and independent woman that I am, I want to decide that for myself and not have him make up my mind for me. Secondly, the man is under a great deal of stress and is currently operating with tunnel vision. Supporting and sustaining his parents, keeping himself together, working at Hamilton and Hamilton and all he is doing for Molly are the equivalent of four full-time jobs. I don't want to be the fifth but nor do I plan to go away quietly.

Fortunately, Amelia Vicars was a remarkably effective diversion.

A slender, timid-appearing woman with pale brown hair, pale gray eyes and wearing a pale yellow dress that resembled an overgrown canvas sack or small pup tent, she greeted me at the door with tepid enthusiasm.

"Mrs. Vicars? I'm Samantha Smith."

"Yes." Apparently she agreed with me on that one.

"We have an appointment today, is that correct?"

"Well, yes." Worry flitted over her features.

"Is there a problem?" There must be since I still hadn't made it past the front door.

"I'm just not sure you can help me…." Amelia wrung her hands like they were soggy dishcloths. "I'm very disorganized."

"Then I'm in the right place. It says in my notes that you want help with your kitchen, is that correct?"

She stepped away from the door and I walked directly into the room in question.

The kitchen was a large, lovely room filled with sunshine. A pair of parakeets put up a noisy ruckus in their cage when we entered. There was not a thing wrong with this kitchen except that every counter, every surface, every square inch of space was filled with food. There were cans of soup, vegetables, fruits, coffee, tuna, beans and juice stacked three high. Cereal boxes were piled five and six high. Rice Krispies was the front-runner. I could count seven boxes from where I stood. Pad thai noodles, vinegar, macaroni, ketchup and wasabi peas need room beside jars of pickles, preserves, pimentos, mayonnaise and peanut butter, mounds of cleaning supplies and an entire case of lemon curd.

"I tend to over-purchase groceries. It's gotten so I don't know where to put them. I thought maybe you could help me."

"Yes, I see." The only quick fix for this would be to serve a week's worth of meals to the men of the United States Army. That might clear it out a bit. "How many people are in your family?"

"Just my husband and me. We have two grown daughters who live in California."

"So this is just for the two of you?" I tiptoed carefully toward the counter. I didn't want to produce any vibrations that might start an avalanche.

"It's a little problem I have. I'm working on it in therapy, but my therapist suggested I call someone like you as well. Can you help me?"

"How long have you been collecting food, Amelia?"

"I quit work three years ago and it seems to have gotten out of hand since then."

"Uh-huh. Three years. Do you have any idea where the food is that you purchased back then or has it all been used up?"

"Well, I really couldn't say." She wrung her dishrag hands again. "I used some, of course, but I always put the new in front so it got mixed up." She stared in horror at her own fecund counters as if they were whelping canned goods as we spoke.

"I suppose I didn't realize how much I had until I ran out of room." She paused in self-amazement. "I had no idea canned goods could fill up a bathtub quickly."

*Okay. Calm down, we don't need to go there—yet.*

I glanced around the room again and made a quick decision. "Amelia, today I'm going to teach you how to read the expiration dates on canned goods."

We spent the next two hours on the floor pulling out cans, reading the expiration dates and either tossing the old food, putting the newer food in boxes for the food shelf and putting "use by" notations on the rest. Visions of botulism were still dancing in my head when I opened the door under the kitchen sink.

I screamed so loudly as the thing jumped out at me that I think I broke two jars of applesauce and the neighbor's window.

"Spider! No… Tumbleweed! No…" I garbled as I scooted backward to get away from whatever was blooming out from beneath the sink. Then I got a whiff of the most foul odor known to kitchens, that of the *rotten potato*.

What I had opened the door upon was a basket full of potatoes, each of which had sprouted and grown a Medusa-like head of potato hair. The long wormy tentacles reaching for me were nothing more than potato sprouts. Or, more accurately, potato sprouts on steroids. Then, having produced this mass of tentacles, the potatoes had melted into smelly little puddles and begun to give off their wretched, odiferous smell.

"Oh, dear," Amelia said behind me. "I'd forgotten all about those."

Obviously. And I'd forgotten my fumigation suit.

This, I thought, as I helped Amelia carry the contents of the entire cupboard on its plastic shelf paper out to the garbage, is why I am going to raise my prices.

Still, by the time I left with nine boxes of food for the food pantry, Amelia was happily arranging what was left of the food and taking the kitchen organizer's oath—

I hereby promise never again to put new cans into my cupboard in front of or on top of old ones. I will make and use a grocery list and check my cupboards *before* I go to the store rather than after I return home. I will no longer load my shelves until they sag and I will begin to trust that there are stores open 24 hours a day if I get hungry. I will buy only what is on my grocery list and if I am tempted to buy French-cut string beans purely because they are being sold 6 cans for a dollar, I will resist. I have difficulty passing up a good sale, therefore, I will go to the store only when absolutely necessary. And if I do not keep this oath, may all my cakes fall in the middle, my vegetables get mushy, my feet grow and every dessert I bake fail.

The oath is tough, I know, but, hey, it's a dirty business. Somebody's got to lay down the law somewhere.

As I drove home, I felt a smile bubbling up from inside me. *Thank You, Lord, for the opportunity to do what I love. I can't believe it, but I even love the smelly stuff. The looks of relief on my clients' faces are so rewarding. Bless Amelia and all her foodstuffs and free her from her compulsion to buy whatever is on sale. You certainly created complex creatures when You created human beings, Lord. The things we can think up! It's just one more sign of how awesome You really are.*

*And Lord, as always, keep Your hand on Molly and her family. If You want Jared and I together, I know You'll make it happen. Show me Your will.*

Zelda was playing jungle cat again. When I walked in the door, I saw her crouching on the top of my armoire, tail flicking, eyes narrowed, scanning the Serengeti horizon for a juicy wildebeest. I saw disappointment in her eyes that I was not the wildebeest she was craving, but she quickly resolved that I would have to do.

She came squealing and yowling off the top of the chest in a launch that would have made Evel Knievel drool, and landed on my shoulder. She nearly gave me a whisker burn with her stubbly shoulder and latched her little white teeth on to the shoulder strap of my purse, the closest thing she could get to wildebeest hide.

"Hi, Zelda, playing again, I see."

Wendy, who was already in the kitchen, clanged two pots together. "She's been on safari ever since I got here. Your plants look like someone took a hedge trimmer to them and there's not a mouse in the house or she would have scarfed it up for you by now."

"I'm glad she entertains herself," I said, plucking the cat off my shoulder and putting her on the floor.

"Imelda entertains herself, too. Did you know she can turn on the television?"

"I taught her."

"Then do you know she likes soap operas and *Judge Judy?* She's crazy about *Wheel of Fortune* and can't stand reruns of *Friends* or *Seinfeld.*"

"Oh, I didn't know she didn't like *Seinfeld.* That must be something new. I usually find her watching *Animal Planet.*" I threw my mail down on the counter.

Wendy, wooden spoon in one hand, stared at me. "I'll never figure out why you want everything so tidy and yet you *encourage* your wacko pets to do whatever it is they do during the day—and you put up with me and Ben, besides."

"Organization is to make life easier, not more difficult. We don't organize for the thrill of it. We do it so that we can enjoy the people and things we have in our life without having our environment be troublesome." I walked across the kitchen and gave Wendy a hug. "I've got my priorities straight, you silly girl."

"And how is Jared doing with his?"

I told Molly about Jared's ill grandfather and the scene Geneva had witnessed, the scene where her father passed the torch to her son, the incident she called "the commissioning."

"At eight years old, Jared was appointed his sister's keeper by a man he loved, a man who was dying," I told Wendy. "That's pretty heavy stuff for a little kid.

"Geneva also told me that her mother always used to remind her husband that, 'If anyone does not provide for his relatives, and especially for his own family, he has disowned the faith and is worse than an unbeliever.' She said Jared was all ears."

"That's an example of using the Word as a club rather than a beckoning hand," Wendy commented. "Responsibility and duty were drilled into him early."

I nodded thoughtfully. "How would you feel if you believed that you had been 'commissioned by' God—and felt you had failed Him? Jared believes he's failed Molly, his grandfather and even God. He's forgetting, of course, that we've all failed God. Romans 3:23—'All have sinned and fall short of the glory of God.'"

Suddenly I thought about my favorite disciple, Peter. If you want to talk about a guy with a directive from God who still managed to fail his Lord, there's one! After that bluster, those good intentions and a somber promise to never deny Christ, what did Peter say when asked if he was one of Jesus' followers? "I do not know what you are talking about… I do not know the man!"

Talk about dropping the ball!

Yet Peter, by God's grace, picked himself up, dusted himself off and became the rock of the church that Christ promised he would. If God could do that for Peter, Jared's issue would be a piece of cake for our loving Lord. But how to convince Jared of that? How to unwind the obligation of a lifetime and put it into God's hands?

I could think of only one answer. By starting to pray for it myself.

## Chapter Twenty-Seven

Zelda has a secret life and it involves a mouse.

No, not *that* kind of mouse. Either she's been researching a kitty dating service on the Internet or ordering catnip by the bale and giving parties while I'm not home. What else could explain her new fascination with my computer?

She's become remarkably computer-literate. I download photos of Zelda and Imelda and use them as screensavers. First I'd found her sitting on my computer chair watching the slide show. Then I realized that when the screen went dark and the computer tried to "sleep," she'd bat the mouse with her paw to wake it up again. She sat with Imelda for hours watching their own pictorial history.

Then, just to give her something new to think about, I added a few photos of strange cats. A Persian, a Siamese and a Russian blue.

It didn't go over well. I think they must have been too hairy for her because I came home to find the cord to my mouse chewed through and the screen dark. I should have learned, but I put a few doggie portraits on so that at least Imelda could continue enjoying her hobby. A sheepdog, a pointer and a setter didn't work well, either. Apparently Imelda doesn't go for the blue-collar, working-dog class. She decimated the cord from my computer tower to the wall plug.

It was after that that I realized they'd somehow called up e-Bay. Maybe it was an accident that happened while Zelda was tripping across the keys, but I've begun shutting my computer down while I'm at work. It's a little freaky. Those two are trouble enough without access to the Internet. Next thing you know, they'd figure out how to get into Paypal and have pet toys and rhinestone collars delivered to the house.

I was brushing Imelda's teeth when I heard the doorbell ring. I went to open the door with the little rubber nubbin-studded doggie toothbrush on my index finger and was so surprised to see Jared outside the hospital, I nearly poked his eye out with the thing.

"What are you doing here?" I said, pointing my encased finger at him.

"I want to talk to you, Sammi. May I come in?" He sounded serious, but that's a difficult frame of mind to retain when my pets are in comic mode.

Imelda ran to within a foot or two of him and smiled.

"What's she baring her teeth at me for? I thought she liked me."

"She does. She's just a canine showing you her clean canines." I waggled my finger. "We got a new toothbrush at the vet today."

He shook his head wearily. "I don't know what planet you three come from sometimes. What's the breed of this dog again? A poo-triever?"

"A labradoodle. And don't make fun of Imelda. She's very sensitive."

At that moment, Zelda, who was sitting regally in the window, gave a magnificent meow of greeting. Jared took one look at her ears, which looked especially large and translucent in the light, and asked, "Is she waiting for the mother ship to come and take her away?"

"If you can't say anything nice about my pets, don't say anything at all," I said, smiling. It was so wonderful to have him here. "Coffee?"

"No. I've had my regulation thirty cups of hospital mud already today."

"Milk? Antacid? I've got fresh chocolate chunk walnut cookies."

He looked both pleased and relieved. "Sure."

I put the pitcher and the cookies on the table and he ate and drank like a starving man. Finally, sated, he looked up. His eyes were bleary and his five o'clock shadow was going on about 11:00 p.m.

"You know just what to do to make me happy, don't you, Sammi?"

"I'd like to think so."

I didn't expect my comment to bring shots of pain to his eyes. "That's why this hurts so much."

I felt a surge of panic in my gut. "What are you talking about?"

"Sammi, you are the most amazing woman in the world but you have come into my life at the worst possible time. You ought to be courted and romanced. All I've been able to do is hope you'll come by the hospital so I can just see you. You've been doing all the giving, and I have been willing to suck you dry just to have you near me. It's not fair. I've been taking you for granted and it's not right. You deserve so much more."

There was an emotional hitch in his voice that frightened me. Whatever conclusions Jared had come to, I had a hunch I wasn't going to like them.

"I can't see my way clear for anything right now, not until

we have a picture of what will happen with Molly. I can't think, I don't sleep…" He raked his fingers through his hair. "Don't hang around waiting for me to figure this out, Sammi. I want so much more for you."

I stared at him in shock and horror. Just like that? Out of the goodness and generosity of his heart he's setting me free? This is the most altruistic reason I've ever heard in a breakup with a man—and also the most ridiculous.

But he means it! He honestly thinks that the most loving act is to send me on my way.

"No, Jared. I couldn't. I wouldn't…"

But the expression on his face told me that, as far as he was concerned, I had no other choice.

*This can't be what You had planned, Lord, is it?*

I felt tears begin to stream down my face.

*Okay, God, I'm speechless. Give me the words You want me to say.*

# Chapter Twenty-Eight

*"You nincompoop!"*

They weren't exactly the words I'd expected from on high, but they got the job done.

Jared blinked and stared at me.

"You sweet, misguided, mistaken man! Freeing me from you would be like opening the door for a bird in a gilded cage," I blustered. "What if the bird likes it just where she's at? What if the cage that you find so confining is the cage she considers 'home'? What if it's where she thrives and sings and feels pampered and loved? Why on earth would a bird like that want to leave? And what kind of a bully does it take to force that bird out into a harsh place she doesn't want to be?"

I was building up a head of steam which finally erupted in a noisy bellow.

"So Jared Hamilton, *quit rattling my cage!*"

Spent, I sat down. I asked for a word from God, and He certainly gave me one.

I looked into Jared's startled countenance and realized that anything else I might have said, pleaded, begged, lectured or counter-offered would have been rejected. But this! I don't know which of us was more surprised, him or me.

He looked at me like I'd just hit him in the face with a plank. Then a small, bewildered smile tipped the corners of his lips and, finally, he started to laugh.

It was infectious and cleansing. As his laughter diluted the tension in his body, I couldn't help joining in. Imelda came over and began to lick my hand, concerned, no doubt, that her mistress was cracking up. Zelda, who enjoys scenes, moved closer just to watch.

We laughed until we cried and then we just cried. For Molly, for her future, for our future. It was a catharsis that purged our fear, frustration, pain and confusion and when we were both exhausted, left us both quiet and calm.

Without a word, Jared gathered me into his arms.

We made our way to the couch without speaking and sat together silently. I could hear the clock ticking on my kitchen wall and Imelda's tongue laving the tops of Jared's shoes. There was even an occasional click of Zelda's tiny jewel-encrusted collar. And Jared's breathing. It was fast at first but as our heartbeats slowed and came into synch, it became un-hurried and deep. As his chest rose and sank, I felt strain leak from his body with each steadying breath. When he finally spoke I heard something in it that had been totally absent since the accident—amusement and relief.

"Okay, my little bird. Apparently you didn't like my sug-gestion. What do *you* think we should do?"

"This is something we go through together. I believe I'm the gift God's giving you for this time in your life, not some helpless Tweety Bird or Chicken Little yelling, 'The sky is falling.'" I fluffed up my emotional feathers as much as any human can do. "I am a *five-hundred-pound canary and I'm here to stay.* So snap out of this sacrificial, altruistic martyrdom and give me a hug!"

"When you chirp, I will listen," Jared said obediently, and he gathered me into his arms—the only cage I ever wanted.

It felt so good to just *be*—together, at peace, in agreement—that neither of us moved for a very long time. Finally, because my foot was falling asleep, I squirmed a little.

"Jared?"

"Hmmm?" The expression on his face was more relaxed than I'd seen since our time at the Oasis.

"Your mother told me about seeing you and your grandfather looking into Molly's crib when you were a child."

His face grew somber. "What did she say?"

"That it sounded as though your grandfather were appointing you to take his place and charging you with the duty of protecting your sister." I hesitated before adding, "Sort of like a voice from above telling a little mortal what's expected of him."

"It was a hard time for me," Jared acknowledged. "I was losing my grandfather, whom I loved very much—and gaining a baby sister. I had it all mixed up, somehow, that God was taking my grandfather away and replacing him with Molly. All I knew was that I had to take good care of Molly or I might lose her, too." He gave a dry, almost bitter laugh. "That shows you how convoluted a child's thinking can be."

"Your mother believes that you took to heart what your grandfather said about your being the one to care for Molly. She knows he didn't mean to 'hand over the torch' or to make you Molly's keeper but that he was trying to tell you how precious she was—for the *entire* family."

"She says that to me regularly." His voice lowered to a near whisper. "Maybe it's true, but I remember that moment with such clarity. It was almost as if it were God giving me those instructions…" He paused. "As if God were giving me those instructions instead of my grandfather…"

"And when Molly got hurt, who did you disappoint? God?"

I could practically see the gears turning in his head

"Unconsciously I have been on a 'mission from God' ever since. That's pretty out there, isn't it?"

"How many times have you bailed Molly out of trouble?"

"Countless. She never hurts anyone else. Only herself."

"So you've been saving her from herself all these years?"

"I suppose so." He laughed humorlessly. "Fat lot of good that's done."

"Jared, what Molly needs is to learn how to save herself from the troubles she gets into."

"And how is that supposed to happen?"

"If she is ADD, there is help. Skills she can learn, medication she can take, professionals she can talk to. Just knowing *why* she functions the way she does might be enough to give her the hope and determination she needs to deal with it."

"And if she's not ADD?"

"Everybody needs hope, Jared. There's a plan for Molly that doesn't have you holding her hand and watching her back."

He looked so doubtful I had to quash a bubble of laughter.

"Jeremiah 29. 'For surely I know the plans I have for you, says the Lord, plans for your welfare and not for harm, to give you a future and a hope.'"

He moved sharply, sending me slightly off balance. "Why are we talking about this? She's lying in a hospital bed unconscious! What makes you think…"

"That she'll recover?"

He winced.

"Because I have hope. And if it doesn't happen, then what do you propose to do about it anyway, except know she's in God's care?"

He buried his head in his hands, and when he spoke his voice was muffled and broken. "I just feel so helpless…."

"You mean until now you've thought you actually had someone to rely on except God? Like yourself?"

He lifted his head and stared at me. "Is that what I've been doing? Handling things for God?"

"I don't know. Have you?"

"You sure know how to hit a guy where it hurts, Sammi. Humility has never been my strong suit."

"God, once He gets a hold on you, starts working on the weak spots, shoring them up to make you stronger in Him."

"Rely on Him, not myself," Jared murmured to himself. "Realize that without Him I'm helpless. That's not an easy request. Especially for a guy like me."

"Competent, smart, successful, proficient, the expert…"

"I was thinking more about thickheaded, vain and doubting."

"Don't be so hard on yourself. You haven't got a monopoly on it, you know. If all those people had to step off the stage, it would be pretty empty."

"You do have a way of bringing things into focus," Jared muttered. "So I'd better get my own act together and trust that God knows what He's doing in Molly's life. And let God take care of both of us…." There was palpable relief in his voice.

He reached to gather me closer and I had to look around to see who was purring. Frankly, I couldn't tell if it was Zelda or *me*. We were both that happy.

Zelda, perched on the back of the couch, moved close enough to Jared to knead her paws into his shoulder and rub the top of her head on his cheek. Imelda had inched closer herself and was still blissfully licking the top of Jared's loafer. It doesn't get much better than this.

"Have you had anything to eat today?" I finally asked. The man needs his stamina if he's going to keep up with me.

"Not much. I had a bag of chips and some cheese and crackers from the vending machine at the hospital for breakfast."

"I know nothing I cook will compare to that, but I'll whip up an omelet. What do you like in it? Mushrooms? Ham? Green pepper?"

I had the frying pan in my hand when Jared's cell phone rang.

He pulled it out of his pocket and flipped it open. "Jared here. What can I do for you...?" He grew white. "Calm down, Ethan, I don't understand you. What? Come to the hospital? What's happened? Ethan, I can't understand you. I'll be right there."

Jared looked up at me with stark terror in his eyes. "Ethan said I was to come to the hospital right away. There were noises in the background, and he was difficult to understand. Something's happened to Molly. I've got to go."

I dropped the pan and Imelda darted for cover. "I'm coming with you."

These tense, fear-filled rides were becoming far too commonplace for us.

"Couldn't you make out anything Ethan said?"

"His voice was trembling," Jared said grimly, "and there was a lot of clatter and noise in the background. There were people talking fast and in high voices."

*Crash cart. Emergency resuscitation. Code blue.* I didn't speak it, but I knew what we were both thinking. Those were potentially noisy things.

"Maybe he stepped into the hall or the cafeteria...."

Jared gave me a well-deserved dirty look. "The cafeteria is on the lower level. He's not going to call me from the cafeteria."

"Maybe it's not too serious," I offered. "Ethan just got rattled."

"Ethan doesn't get rattled," Jared said bluntly. "Other than that scene in his office when I met you, I've never seen him out of control of anything."

That day seemed so long ago and deeply mired in the

distant past that it was difficult even to conjure it up. I hadn't loved Jared then. I hadn't even liked him. How times do change.

"Slow down," I said almost automatically. "Whatever is going on, Ethan is there. And your parents. They'll have to handle it."

"It's hard, letting go," Jared murmured. "Especially if it might be forever. Lord," he murmured, not talking to me but to the other One with us in the car. "I've hung on to everything—Molly, my duty to her, my idea that she can't get along without me. And now You are showing me that I haven't been in control of anything, even for a minute. I release everything I've been trying to control. It is in Your hands now. If You see fit to spare Molly, I praise You. And if You don't…"

A long, painful silence ensued. Finally I heard him murmur softly, "If You don't see fit to spare her, then I praise You, too."

Tears coursed down my cheeks as we made the rest of our silent ride to the hospital.

# Chapter Twenty-Nine

I've seen albino rabbits with more color than Jared had in his face by the time we were in the elevator and on our way to Molly's room.

*Lord, whatever is, is. Put Your healing hand upon this situation and please gift us with the "peace that passes understanding." We could use a good helping of that. May Your name be praised. Amen.*

The door to Molly's room was closed. Confused, we looked at a passing nurse, who gave a quick brush of her hand as if to say, "Go in. What are you waiting for?"

Jared's hands were clenched and unmoving at his sides so I reached out and gave the door a small shove. It opened onto a scene of chaos. We remained frozen in our places as Ben, wearing a pair of fake glasses, the kind with eyeballs popping out on the end of small springs, waved us in.

"What on earth?" I stepped between him and Jared so that Jared did not attempt to smack him for looking so ridiculous when his sister was on her deathbed.

"Sssshhh," Ben hissed. "The doctor is trying to explain it to your parents."

"Explain? You mean how she…" Jared choked on the unspoken word.

"Yeah. We all wanted to know."

"Vultures," Jared spat.

"I don't think so," Ben said as he stared at Jared in bewilderment. "The only bird in this room looks to me like a loon."

"Let me by." Jared pushed Ben aside and strode toward his mother who was standing at the foot of Molly's bed. The divider curtain hid his sister from view.

"Mom, I'm so…"

He stopped, and his shoulder jerked as if he'd been punched. "Wha—" His voice dropped to a whisper. "Molly?"

"She opened her eyes about thirty minutes ago," Ben explained to me in a low voice. "She's coming back to us. Molly is coming back."

Illogically, I went to the least important issue at hand. "Us?"

Ben grimaced. "Yes, *us*. To me, too. Is that what you're asking?"

I gaped at him, still in shock.

His eyeballs, all four of them, rolled. "I was showing her some magic tricks. I was about to pull a hamster out of a hat when she opened her eyes!"

It's a wonder that she didn't take a look at Ben and faint again. His hair bristled out of his head in a hundred directions, his cheeks were flushed and those eyes…so many of them and so loosely attached to his head… And did he have a *hamster* in here somewhere?

He beamed at me and I saw for the first time something I probably should have noticed much earlier—amazingly, astoundingly, all this time Ben has been coming to "help out," he's been falling in love!

"Ben, what's going on with you and—" I felt ridiculous saying it "—Molly?"

He bit his lip and I saw that my exploratory arrow had hit its target. "She's been like a doll laying there, Sammi, a beautiful, soft-haired, fragile cherub. Every time someone speaks about her, it's in terms of her generosity, her love, her *goodness*." He smiled a little. "And her messiness. I like that in a woman."

"So you began to think about how it would be to have that kind of woman in your life, that kind of woman to love." Strangely, I understood.

"And I'd never even 'met' her, but I found myself praying for her to recover, to wake up, to be healed." He blushed to the roots of his hair. "And to her future."

"And yours?"

"If God wills it."

"God works in mysterious ways." We were all proof of that.

"No kidding."

Ben took me by the arm and thrust me into the crowd around Molly. Jared, Molly's parents, Ethan, three doctors and a bevy of nurses ringed the bed. Jared reached out his hand and drew me in.

She lay there blinking owlishly and appearing bemused. The bruise on her head was almost healed and she looked utterly Molly-like. Then she saw me, and a smile spread slowly across her face. With great effort, she lifted her hand as if to reach out for me and her mouth struggled around a single word. "Sam."

That was it for me. I burst into tears and blurted, "Molly, welcome home! We've missed you."

Her answering smile seemed to say she understood perfectly.

Things became hazy for me after that. The doctors shooed us out of the room so they could evaluate Molly and we stood in the hallway crying and laughing. Then the nurses steered us into the family room to keep us from disturbing the entire hospital with our celebration. Ultimately we all retired to the cafeteria to swill back iced tea and laugh, cry and make a general spectacle of ourselves. It was glorious.

"So what happened," I demanded. "What *really* happened?"

"Molly's father and I have been here all day. I read to her from the newspaper as I always do and treated her like she was 'in there' somewhere." A tear spilled down Geneva's cheek. "If there was any chance at all that she could hear us, she had to know how much she is loved."

"Then Ben came along with a paper bag full of magic tricks and his usual candy bar," Robert said.

"Candy bar?" Jared and I chimed together.

"He's got this shtick," Mr. Hamilton continued, "Every time he comes, he lays a salted peanut roll, Molly's favorite, on the foot of the bed."

"How'd you know what her favorite candy was?" Jared wanted to know.

"He asked." Leave it to Ben to cut to the chase. "Anyway, Geneva and I always laugh because he'd say, 'Molly, if you wake up while I'm here, you get this candy bar. If you don't, I'm going to eat it right in front of you. So if you know what's good for you…' and he'd make a big deal of the candy and then, of course, have to eat it before he left.

"The last few days we've been noticing responses in her. Although the doctors said it could just be reflex actions, we thought we saw her smile."

"It seemed like she smiled a little more each time Ben came," Geneva added.

"And today, when Ben was about to leave and went to eat the candy bar, she opened her eyes and said, 'No!'"

"I walked in just about time this happened," Ethan said, picking up the story. "And that's when I called you and told you to get yourself over here."

Jared sagged in his chair. "And because it was so noisy in

the background and I didn't hear all you said, I thought something terrible had happened and she had died."

Ethan looked anguished at the thought. "I'm so sorry, buddy. Everyone was talking and running in and out. I never dreamed you didn't hear all I said."

"Well, it turned out all right. Better I suffer a little than Molly." He was still willing to take the pain for the people he loved.

Ethan looked relieved.

"Now what?" Jared asked. "Does she hop out of bed and everything goes back to normal?"

"Hardly," his mother said. "But if, as the doctors think, her mind is good, they'll start her on physical therapy to help her get her strength back. They won't give us any estimates on how long it might take, but they believe that we will have our Molly back." And Geneva, relieved of the strain and fear that had been weighing on her, began to sob.

It was after eight when Jared finally dropped me off at my place. We were both wrung out, having been dragged through a knothole on an emotional toothpick. But the world seemed brighter, the colors more vivid, the birds louder and our hearts were bursting with relief and gratitude.

He brushed his index finger across my cheek. The movement seemed to cost him the last of his energy. "Shall I stop by for you tomorrow? Now that I know Molly is safe, I need to try to pick up the pieces of her business. She'll have *me* fired if she knows how lax I've been."

"But with good reason," I reminded him gently. "It's time for you to stop overprotecting her and bailing her out, Jared. Molly's a survivor, we all know that for sure now. If I know anything at all about your sister, it's that she'll come back from this charging straight ahead, tackling whatever comes in her way."

"I wish I were so brave," he murmured.

"You are. You've carried an impossible burden ever since you were eight years old, a misguided commission from your grandfather. You've been trying to do God's work for Him where Molly is concerned. He just showed us He can handle her on His own."

"Touché," he admitted. A slow smile spread across his handsome features. "But if Molly's handled, what am I going to do with my time? Who will I take care of...and love?"

I leaned over and kissed him on the cheek. "I'll help you think of someone."

# Chapter Thirty

Once she began to emerge from the coma, Molly's functionality increased and she progressed rapidly in therapy and her recovery. She insisted on going home as soon as possible.

"Hiya, sis," Jared greeted her as we walked into her living room. He bent to give her a kiss on the cheek before he spied her visitor. "You? Here *again?* Is there something we should know about the two of you?" The picture Aunt Gertie had taken was sitting on the bedside table. Ironically, Molly was the only one who'd recognized immediately what it was.

"Is this guy giving you any trouble?" he asked his sister. "You want me to punch his lights out?"

Molly grinned and grabbed Ben's hand as if to protect him. "Mine," she said firmly. "Leave him alone."

"Geneva had an appointment," Ben explained. "I'm filling in."

"You seem to be here 'filling in' here all day long. What do we hire caregivers for, anyway?" Jared asked, grinning. "Don't you have work to do?"

Ben pointed to a bunch of dreary-looking books and ring binders. "I brought it with me."

It seems that Molly, in her semiconscious state, actually *had* been aware of much of the conversation around her in the hospital. For whatever reason, it was Ben's voice that had come through most loud and clear.

It still seemed to be the one getting her attention.

When Ben and Jared disappeared into the kitchen to see what was in the refrigerator, I sat down beside Molly and took her hand in mine.

"How are you doing today?"

"Good. The doctor says I'm amazing." Her words were slower and more studied now and she didn't…couldn't …waste time in idle chatter.

"I've always said that." I glanced over my shoulder toward the kitchen. "What's going on here? Anything I should know about?"

Her eyes glazed with tears. Her emotions are nearer the surface these days, as well. "I think I love him."

Of all the answers I'd been expecting, it hadn't been that.

"You haven't known him very long." *And most of the time you were unconscious.*

"I *know* him. I heard him."

Ben's voice is distinct and musical and to Molly he'd been a Pied Piper, luring her back to the land of the living.

"Are you telling me that you and Ben are an item?"

The weight she'd lost after the accident had left attractive hollows in her cheeks which highlighted her excellent bone structure. She beamed at me. "We're in love."

"In love? You and Ben? How…what…?"

"I already feel as if I know him quite well, Sammi. He talked to me for hours about his family, The Timer, quantum physics…"

"And he knows you through your family and friends." Put that way, it made sense.

*Be My Neat-Heart*

Jared sauntered into the living room looking relaxed and happy. That man is so handsome that it should be illegal.

"Ben went to the grocery store," he told Molly. "He says he knows exactly what you like."

Hmmm. If Ben already knows Molly's likes and dislikes…
"Jared, what are *my* favorite foods?"

He looked at me blankly. "Is this a test?"

"You could call it that. Ben knows Molly's favorites, I thought you might know mine." I struggled not to add "or else."

Abruptly I was sorry I'd started the conversation. What if he didn't have a clue? I'd set myself up to be hurt and insulted.

It took forever for him to answer. When he did, my shoulders sagged in relief.

"Oreos, hot cocoa, chocolate bars, anything Godiva, Cocoa Puffs in chocolate milk, fudge cake, chocolate chip cookies and pretty much anything else that has chocolate in it. You have a sweet tooth the size of New York City, never gain a pound and women everywhere would give anything for your metabolism. You also like steak, lobster, clams, shrimp, pork chops, mashed potatoes, burgers and fries. In fact, you just love food except for rutabaga, smelly cheese, veal, lamb, wild game and tomato aspic. And you could put a man in the poor house with an appetite like yours."

He leaned back and crossed his arms over his chest. "Fortunately, I'm not just any man and I am definitely not poor."

Molly clapped as the color rose in my cheeks.

Knowing he'd made big points with me, Jared continued as if we'd never had this little digression. "Now, what were you talking about when I walked into the room?"

"Molly's in love," I blurted.

He looked at her doubtfully. "When did you have time to fall in love? You've been unconscious."

"Not exactly," I corrected. "Tell him, Molly."

And she did.

When Ben returned with the groceries, Jared greeted him with a slap on the back that made Ben nearly dropped the food sacks. I rescued the groceries and announced that Jared and I would cook lunch while he sat with Molly.

"Can you believe it's true?" Jared puzzled as he cut fresh fruit onto a plate. "Ben and Molly, head over heels in love? Maybe there's a medical explanation for what's happened to her. She seems so sure…."

"A medical explanation for love? Come on!"

"I suppose I shouldn't think I know what goes on in Molly's mind now, either," he said with a sigh. "I had no clue before the accident, and now… Maybe Ben is the best thing that's ever happened to my sister."

I started spreading butter on thick slabs of bread and piling them with turkey. "You heard what she said. Her disorganization doesn't bother him a bit. He thinks it's charming."

Jared shuddered. "Ben must have had a clunk on his head, too."

When we brought the food to them, they were holding hands and staring at each other with goofy grins on their faces.

"So I hear you think Molly's disorganization is charming, huh, Ben?" Jared said bluntly. "Do you really know what you're getting into?"

I tried to elbow him in the side and to quiet him but Jared dodged me with the agility of a wide receiver.

"That's right, Jared," Molly said complacently. "You don't have to worry about my messes anymore because you're marrying Sammi, not me."

I tensed. How would Jared respond to that?

"I am, am I?" His tone was carefully bland and noncommittal.

"Jared," Molly said patiently as she put her sandwich to her lips. "Don't be an idiot and mess this up. I don't want any sister-in-law at all if I can't have Sammi."

Where's a water tank to cool my flaming cheeks in when I really need it?

I decided to keep my mouth shut as we drove away from Molly's. Jared had grown quiet after her startling statement and it worried me. Had I been composing a fairy tale about us while he'd been inventing an entirely different ending to our story?

I'd thrown my policy of "better safe than sorry" out the window and look where it had gotten me. In mortal danger of a broken heart.

I was so busy beating myself up for being a fool that I didn't realize at first that he'd driven to Minnehaha Falls rather than my house.

I love the falls. There are shelters and picnic tables nearby and almost invariably, there is a wedding party or two having their pictures taken with the falls in the background.

In fact, a bride and groom and their attendants were just piling into limousines when we arrived.

Brides are much younger these days, I've noticed. This one looked as though she were barely pushing twelve years old. Or is that what happens when one reaches thirty? Anyone younger begins to look like a toddler playing dress-up.

One of the groomsmen brushed by me on his way to the car and a question bubbled up inside me. I couldn't help myself. It just came out.

"Excuse me, but how old are the bride and groom?"

He looked at me strangely but he answered politely enough. "They just graduated from college. They're twenty-two and twenty-three."

"Oh. Thank you."

So they were of legal age. It was me who was getting toward the age when it shouldn't be legal to be single.

"What's wrong? You look as if you just had bad news." Jared looked down into my eyes, concerned. "Don't you like it here?"

"I love it. I'm having a minicrisis. Do you know how young that couple in the limo looks?"

"They're in their early twenties, I imagine."

*So what does that make me? Grandma Moses?*

Wishing I'd had a walker or a cane to stagger to the falls with, I gloomily took Jared's hand and followed him to the large stones where we could sit and look down on the water. I felt a spray of mist on my face as the wind shifted, and was transported back to all the times I'd visited here as a child...so long ago...in the dark ages...when dinosaurs roamed the earth...and I was young.

"What on earth is bugging you, Sammi?" Jared put his finger beneath my chin and lifted it, forcing me to look at him.

"It's just dumb. Never mind."

"I've learned that nothing is ever 'dumb' with you. I'm willing to sit here all day until you're ready to talk."

Sitting here all day didn't sound like a bad idea, but I'm not built to remain quiet for long. Emotions and opinions don't easily stay unspoken.

"Molly and Ben—in love! And those children in the limousines—they should still have curfews! What's happening to this world? It's going so fast. My life is going so fast."

"Getting old quickly, are you?"

That was *not* the question I wanted him to ask.

"So are you," I retorted. "And what are we going to do about it?"

"There isn't much we can 'do' about it."

"So you're just going to sit placidly around getting old?"

"I take it this isn't exactly about age, is it?"

I wish he'd quit smiling at me like I was some big form of entertainment for him. "Of course it is...not."

"And if we could do something about how quickly time flies, what would it be?"

Oh great. Now he's a philosopher.

"I don't know. Make it the best time. Not waste it." *Not sit around on rocks and wish for something to happen.*

"And how would that be?"

I felt myself getting sucked in to his questions. "Have fun? Laugh? Worship? Eat chocolate?"

"What else?"

"I'd ski, I suppose. And travel. And surround myself with friends and family. My parents and brothers, of course. And Aunt Gertie and her husband, Arthur. Wendy, Ben and Molly."

"Anyone else?"

"Ideally, children, I suppose. And a husband. And more pets. A pot-bellied pig or a miniature goat."

Jared winced. "A husband and a miniature goat. I see. Where would you get the goat?"

If he was trying to distract me, it was working.

"The woman who runs the pet store I go to, Norah's Ark, has connections. She probably knows of three or four goats right now that need good homes."

"So the goat is no problem?"

"Not really. Other than I'd need a bigger lawn. Maybe I'd have to buy a bigger house."

"And what about the husband? Where do you go for one of those?"

I snorted—not ladylike, but effective at showing distain. "I'd probably have to advertise in the newspaper." *Husband wanted to father children and care for goat.*

Suddenly Jared's arm was close around me and I was tucked neatly into his chest and couldn't squirm away. His breath warmed my cheek and I could see every fleck of violet in those blue eyes of his.

"So where would I go to apply for the job? Of goat keeper and husband, I mean."

"Well, since I have a small yard, I don't need a goat quite yet...."

"And a husband?"

My pulse was racing and the heat of his hand at my waist seared my skin.

"I think I'd need him before I got the goat and the children."

"I see. Do you have an application form I could fill out? I don't have any references since I've never been married, but maybe my mother and my sister could write up a little something about my sterling character."

"I don't need references," I murmured, the roar of the falls and of my heart pounding in my ears. "But the job requirements include being a good kisser. Are you up to that?"

"May I audition right now?" His head tipped forward toward mine.

"I have the time, I guess."

"Good," he whispered, and gave the best audition of his life.

## Chapter Thirty-One

After seeing each other for several months, Molly and Ben decided to follow us to the altar.

My mother was a little confused at first. She couldn't get it out of her mind that I should be marrying Ben instead of Jared.

"But you've known Ben for five years, darling. You've known Jared for less than a year. That's not like you. When did you start throwing caution to the wind?"

It would have taken longer to explain that than it did for Jared and me to fall in love. Let's face it, I'm *not* like me anymore. I'm better.

God has worked absolute miracles in my life and in those of the rest of the wedding party. Jared is free, for the first time in nearly thirty years, from feeling that he needs to protect Molly from herself. Molly is alive, which is miracle enough. And Ben has found a soul mate. I suppose this wasn't one of God's most complicated situations, but it was plenty complex for us. Only He could have sorted it out.

Aunt Gertie and Arthur came to our wedding, of course. After the wedding, Aunt Gertie, a cheek pincher, grabbed Jared by the face and told him that if I wasn't going to marry

Ben, then he was definitely the next best choice. It's interesting that the only two people who didn't assume Ben and I would marry one day were Ben and I.

Aunt Gertie forgave us both, I know. She brought us matching gifts, a wedding present for Jared and me, an engagement gift for Ben and Molly. Now Jared and I and Molly and Ben will each have a chair in the shape of a high-heeled shoe for our living rooms. Ours is pink and black while Ben and Molly's is a garish red. Jared had a pretty horrified look on his face at the sight of it until I reminded him of how much Imelda loves shoes. She should have it eaten in no time.

"Leaving so soon?" Ben asked. "The reception is just getting started."

It had actually been in full swing for some hours but Ben, obviously, was having a first-rate time. His new love hadn't let him out of her sight for hours.

"It's nearly midnight," Jared said. "We're catching a flight to Hawaii at six a.m. You keep the party going. We've already said our goodbyes." He clapped Ben on the back. "Take care of her for me, will you…." He paused as he caught my warning expression. "That's right, no more assigning duties. May God take care of *both* of you. He can handle it."

Ben gathered me in his arms and gave me a bear hug. "It's perfect, Sammi, soon we'll be in-laws and you'll never be able to get rid of me."

I squeezed back a tear. "Nor will I ever want to."

We arrived at the door to my house where Jared swept me off my feet and carried me across the threshold. Then he set me down and kissed me soundly until the tips of my toes started to tingle.

"Here we are, Mrs. Hamilton. Home together at last." He

looked around. "It's awfully quiet in here. What do you think they're up to?"

"'They'? As in Zelda and Imelda? Probably sleeping. It's past their bedtimes." I sighed. "I hope they're okay while we're gone. Wendy promised me she'd take care of them like they were her own. Knowing Wendy, that's not all that comforting."

A single yip came from the direction of the kitchen.

"Wha—" We went to the doorway of the kitchen that Wendy—it couldn't have been anyone else—had blocked off with a pet gate. Beyond the gate were Zelda and Imelda, dressed for a wedding celebration.

Zelda wore a new collar with little bride and groom charms on it and a white sweater on which Wendy had stitched a plethora of white sequins. The cat looked as though she were imitating the Queen Mum.

Imelda was equally fitted out in bridal wear. She had a plastic tiara attached to the fur on her head and a fluffy white tutu hanging off her haunches. Wendy had appliquéd little silver shoes onto the netting. She yipped again and I would have bet a million dollars that they were posing just for us. On the table behind them was a miniature wedding cake with a sign sprouting out of the cake. "Warning—made of cottage cheese and tuna fish. Party on."

A half hour later, as Zelda and Imelda lay sleeping at our feet, satiated, Jared and I curled together on the couch.

"Now I can leave assured that Wendy will take care of them," I admitted. "I underestimated her. They may not even want me back."

"Oh, I think they'll be pleased." Jared tipped my face toward his and kissed the tip of my nose. "I know I'm thrilled to know I'm spending the rest of my life with you."

"Are you?" I teased. "I'm a little high maintenance—the pets, my business, the cleaning fixation and all."

"You don't think I can do 'high maintenance'? After Molly, living with you will be a walk in the park." He planted a kiss on my ear that I felt in my kneecaps. "Besides, I've been warned."

"By who?" I sat straight up. "If it's Wendy, she's lying. Don't believe a word of it."

He took me by the shoulders and turned me toward him. "*You* warned me, darling."

"Me? I haven't said a word."

"You didn't need to. I hired you to help me organize my sister's life, and you turned my life into chaos. I ended up with a wife, a new brother-in-law, an extended family and a pair of wacko animals who think they're human. Not only that, I'm spending my wedding night eating a cottage-cheese cake with a dog in a tutu and a cat wearing sequins and rhinestones. You've threatened to buy a goat and have a half-dozen children. Don't you think I've realized by now that you are not an ordinary woman and I've signed up for a life of pandemonium?"

"That does sound like a lot." I tucked myself a little closer to my new husband. "Fortunately for you, I'm good at sorting out complex situations. What part of your life would you like me to organize for you?"

"Not a thing, darling, not a thing. I think we've finally reached perfection."

* * * * *

Dear Reader,

*Be My Neat-Heart* was a pleasure to write for many reasons. It is such fun to create characters that not only cherish their Christian faith, but also enjoy a good sense of humor. Laughter is a gift to be relished.

In the nonwriting part of my life, I am a personal life coach, so making my very organized heroine Samantha Smith a clutter coach seemed a natural thing to do.

I also understand Molly's side of the story. As a creative person, I'm very visual. And that, in my office, often translates into messy. If one's home is an outward manifestation of one's inward emotional state and we're looking at my office, I'm in big trouble. I'm always trying to master the paper and books I live with. To write a story about a clutter coach and her very frustrating client taps into two of my most familiar experiences.

I'm working on a master's degree in human development in the areas of writing, coaching and spirituality. *Be My Neat-Heart* has been a playful intersection of these three spheres. I hope you have as much fun with the characters as I have.

Blessings,

*Judy*

# QUESTIONS FOR DISCUSSION

1. Is it true that external clutter reflects inner turmoil in a person's life? Can you think of examples from your own life?

2. Whom did you identify with in this story and why? Did you recognize anyone you know in the characters on the page?

3. Which character was it most difficult for you to relate to?

4. How does what happens in this story relate to your life?

5. Did you realize what Molly's problem really was or did it come as a surprise to you? Why?

6. Would you ever hire a clutter coach? What could he or she do for you that you aren't doing for yourself right now?

7. Have you ever been to a spa like the one Samantha goes to? What did you enjoy most about it?

8. Have you ever felt like you've been expected by God to do something very important and been unable to achieve it? How did it make you feel?

9. If you were going to give someone two of your best tips for keeping your life and home in order, what would they be?

10. What do you believe God expects of us in regard to our possessions and the care of them?

*Turn the page for a sneak preview of*
*NORAH'S ARK by Judy Baer.*
*On sale in September 2006*
*from Steeple Hill Café.*

# Welcome to Norah's Ark

## *Have You Hugged Your Iguana Today?*

Norah Kent, owner/operator of
Norah's Ark Pet Store and
Doggie B&B (Bed and Biscuit)

I stood back and studied the sign I'd placed in the window. Creative marketing for a pet store has its own unique challenges. It's hard to know, really, if an iguana will lend itself to the same "isn't that cute" factor as my *Cuddle a puppy tonight!* campaign had. It would help if I had an extra dime to spend on professional advice, but I usually have at least a hundred and fifty extra mouths to feed and that adds up. Granted, the fish and birds don't take much, but the mastiff puppies I'm currently housing make up for it.

"New Monday morning promotion, Norah? What will it be next, 'Grin at Your Guppy' or 'Tickle Your Toad'?"

I didn't have to turn around to know it was Joe Collier from the Java Jockey, the coffee shop and hangout down the street from my pet store.

"What do you think?"

"Makes me think I'd rather hug *you*."

"Get a grip, Joe, this is important business." I didn't turn around to look at him because I knew he was serious and I didn't want to encourage him. Joe's been pursuing me ever since the day I and my menagerie moved into the storefront near him two years ago.

I left a perfectly nice, secure, decent-paying job managing a veterinary clinic and being a veterinarian's assistant to pursue a dream of owning my own business, and not even hunky, persistent Joe is going to derail me now.

"When are you going to ease up, Norah? Norah's Ark has as much walk-in traffic as my coffee shop."

I turned around to look at him. Joe is six foot two inches tall, has curly black hair, pale blue eyes and the best muscles a lifetime membership at the sweatiest gym in town can buy. He always wears a white, long-sleeved shirt with the cuffs rolled up his forearms, jeans and loafers without socks. That's no easy feat in Minnesota during the winter, but Joe's a guy for all seasons.

"There's no time for a small business owner to 'ease up.' You know that." I waved my arm, gesturing at the rows of businesses housed in quaint, former Victorian homes flanking both sides of Pond Street. Pond Street was named, tongue-in-cheek, because it runs directly into Lake Zachary, one of the largest, most populated and popular boating lakes in the city. In fact, every street in Shoreside runs directly toward the lake, like spokes on a bicycle. The avenues, which would normally run in the opposite direction, are more in an every-man-for-himself pattern. The slightly rolling terrain and difficulty of finding one's way around town only made it more appealing to people. Over the years, Shoreside has become an exclusive and trendy—if confusing—place to live.

"None of us would be here if we 'eased up.'" The summer traffic here is great but winters can be slow. We have to work when the sun shines—literally.

"So just slip out for a couple hours this Saturday night and I'll introduce you to this great Italian restaurant I know. Think of it as an opportunity to pay tribute to my maternal ancestors. What do you say?"

Joe has a smile so beguiling that it can melt ice cubes. If I don't give myself some space to think, I succumb to it every time.

"I'll let you know later."

"Not much later, I hope," he teased. "I have a whole list of other beautiful women to ask out if you turn me down." His dimples dimped—or whatever it is dimples do—but I still resisted. "I'll tell you after I close the store tonight, okay?"

"You're a hard sell, Norah. Maybe that's why I like you." He chucked me under the chin like he does my dog Bentley, and sauntered back to the coffee shop.

If he thinks my hard-to-get persona is attractive, that means that saying "no" is only going to fuel his fire. I'll have to think of a new tactic to keep him at bay.

It's not that I don't like Joe. I do. Almost too much. The problem is that I'm just not *ready* for Joe. He wants a serious girlfriend, someone with marriage potential who is ready to settle down, and I'm not that girl—yet. Sometimes I worry that he might not be willing to wait.

Still, I love owning my own business and being independent and I want to have that experience for a while longer. I'm a throw-myself-into-something-with-total-abandon kind of girl. When I marry, I'll be the most enthusiastic wife and homemaker ever, but right now that something is the shop. Besides, although I've never admitted it to another living soul, I think I'm waiting for bells to chime, to feel the poke of Cupid's arrow as it lands in my backside, or sense a shimmery-all-over feeling that I imagine I'll have when I fall in love. It's my personal secret that I feel this way. Everyone thinks I'm a sensible realist. Hah! Nothing could be further from the truth.

I decided to leave the iguana sign up for a day or two to test the response, and was about to reenter the store when Auntie Lou came out the front door of her store to sweep the sidewalk. Surreptitiously, I watched as she tidied up the front of Auntie Lou's Antiques. Her name is actually Louella

Brown, and her age is…well, somewhere over a hundred and fifty, I think. Auntie Lou is the oldest antique in her shop, cute as a bug and wrinkled as a raisin. She also dyes her hair a fire-engine red-orange that makes Lucille Ball's and Carrot Top's tresses look anemic. This morning had her distinctive hair tucked under a cloche hat, and she wasn't wearing her upper plate, so she looked especially raisinlike. Still, I found her smile appealing when she waved me over for a visit.

"How's my pretty today?" Auntie Lou asked. She always says that. When she does, I immediately flash back to Dorothy and the Wicked Witch of the West in *The Wizard of Oz*. If I had a dog named Toto, I'd grab him and run.

"Great, how are you?"

"Arthur kept pestering me all night and Ruma-tiz, too. Those boys are pure trouble."

Translation: her arthritis and rheumatism are acting up again.

"Sorry to hear that."

"Oh, to be young and pretty like you!" Auntie Lou reached out and touched a strand of my long, dark hair which is currently in one of its wilder stages.

I inherited my naturally curly hair from my mother, who, no matter how hard she tries, can't get those kinks and waves next to her scalp to settle down. Mom's blond and beautiful and has settled for an upswept "do" that corrals and tames it fairly well. I, on the other hand, have let my dark hair grow as long as it will and usually harness it into a whale spout sort of ponytail that erupts from near the top of my head and hangs to somewhere between my shoulder blades. People—especially kids—want to touch my hair to see if it's real.

My mom also has remarkable gray-green eyes, which, happily, I also inherited. As a child, I would look into her eyes and felt as if I could actually see her tender heart enshrouded in that smoky gray-green haze. My dad says I have the same eyes "only more so." He insists I actually wear my heart on my sleeve and it's my entire soul that is on display in my eyes. It's an interesting concept, but I try not to think about it. I'm not sure there's a good mascara sold to enhance one's soul.

I *am* a big softy. This much is true. I'm a total pushover for children, the elderly and anyone who is an underdog or down on his luck. However, I am also a complete and total sucker for anything with four feet, fur, gills, wings, claws, tails or webbed feet. I volunteer as a willing midwife to anything that gives birth in litters, broods or batches. I love tame and wild, pedigreed and mutt alike. I've been this way since the first time I grabbed our golden retriever Oscar by the tail as a tiny child and he licked my face instead of giving me the reprimanding nip I deserved.

My parents still remind me of the Christmases I'd cry when I saw a doll under the tree instead of stuffed animals, and the bucket of oats and toddler swimming pool I kept filled with fresh water in the backyard "just in case a pony comes by." I rode the back of our velvet floral print couch as if it were a bucking bronco until my plastic toy spurs shredded a pillow and I was banished to pretending to ride a horse around the backyard. I must have looked deranged, now that I think of it, whooping and slapping myself on the butt to make myself go faster. Good thing I didn't own any sort of crop or whip.

My dad is a veterinarian and my mom a nurse, so there was usually something with wings or paws bandaged up and living at our house while it mended. In fact, I assumed that everyone had a pet snake until I took mine to my friend's house to show her mother how pretty he looked now that he'd shed his old skin. That, I was quick to discover, was a very bad assumption. She did forgive me, however, as soon as the paramedic revived her.

Anyway, I'm a softy for all the unique characters on Pond Street, too.

"You got a good mouser over there?" Auntie Lou inquired. "I'm in need of a shop cat, a working feline. How much will it cost me?"

"Not much. I'll drive you to the animal shelter tonight and we'll find something perfect for you. I think a calico kitten would be a great accessory for your antiques. He'd sleep on that soft cushion on the platform rocker in the window…."

"How do you make a living, Norah? I want to *buy* a cat from you."

"Let's adopt a kitten and I'll sell you a kitten bed, food, toys, catnip and a scratching post instead."

Auntie Lou shook her head helplessly.

"And I'll make you sign a paper saying you'll buy him a lifetime supply of food from my store, if that will make you happy."

"Done, you silly child." Auntie Lou patted me on the cheek and turned to reenter her shop.

I like to consider myself an adoption agency, not a pet store. I *place* animals in homes. I spend time with prospective pet owners helping them decide what type of pet is best for them and then help them find the perfect one. I've even considered adding "pet consultant" behind my name. Dad says I'm nuts, but I actually make a great living selling all the pet accessories people need for their perfect pet. I have a very loyal following—all people as nutty about animals as I am. I also run the Doggie B&B—Bed & Biscuit—out of the back of the shop for loyal customers who want to travel and have their pets in a safe and familiar place. The business keeps growing, especially now that I include all pets, not just dogs, and have begun serving homemade birthday cakes to those who celebrate their special day away from family. Once a customer caught me and his beagle wearing paper birthday hats and together howling out an eardrum-splitting rendition of "Happy Birthday to You." Needless to say, I got a huge tip and a lifetime fan. Only animal people understand these things.

Of course, I do have the usual pet-store animals in my store—at least two of everything, just like Genesis 7:8 "Of clean animals and of animals that are not clean, and birds, and of everything that creeps on the ground, two and two, male and female, went into the ark with Noah, as God had commanded Noah." Except the rabbits, of course. I always start with just two, but, well, they *are* rabbits after all. Anyway, if it was good enough for God and Noah, it's good enough for me.

I've been a Christian since I was ten years old. As a child, I was drawn to all the verses of the Bible that refer to God's four-legged creatures. Even the most lowly, a donkey, for instance, held significance for Christ. When He rode into the city of Jerusalem, He didn't do so on a chariot. Instead, He came humbly, a serene, peace-desiring king on a donkey's unbroken colt. "Go into the village ahead of you…you will find tied there a colt that has never been ridden: untie it and bring it. If anyone says to you, 'Why are you doing this?' just say this, 'The Lord needs it….'" The commonplace becomes exceptional when God is involved.

Everyone, it seemed, was having a difficult time staying indoors on a beautiful day like this. Next out of her store was Lilly Culpepper, our local fashion maven. Lilly and I moved onto Pond Street and opened our little shops within a few weeks of each other and have ridden the up and down the roller-coaster ride of small-business ownership together ever since.

She runs a funky clothing store called The Fashion Diva next to Norah's Ark and is a walking advertisement for the things she sells in her shop. Today she wore a long, red Santa

Fe-style crinkle pleated skirt, a short boxy sweatshirt the color of old mushrooms, high heeled black boots and a gray felt fedora. And it looked good. I wonder how many hopeful shoppers leave her store with similar outfits hoping that they'll look like Lilly when they get home and put their new clothes on. And I wonder how many of those shoppers realize that at home, those same clothes look like the pile of wrinkled, mismatched laundry they already have lying on their closet floor.

What Lilly doesn't—and can't—sell is her style. She looks good even in a gunnysack and a pair of galoshes. I know this for sure because one year we went to a costume party as a sack of potatoes and potato fork. She looked great and I looked as though I'd been wrapped in brown crepe paper and had a set of pronged antlers strapped to my head. Next time *I* get to be the vegetable.

"Joe asking you out again?" She greeted me with no preamble. Though she came nearer, she didn't walk toward me. Lilly doesn't walk, Lilly *sweeps*.

Anyway, as she swept toward me I said, "Good morning to you, too."

"If you'd say the word, he'd get down on bended knee and ask for your hand in marriage."

"My hand isn't much good to him without the rest of me."

"You could do worse," she advised me. She fingered the chunk of jewelry at her neck. It was a hodgepodge of beads, colored cubes, macramé lumps and various ribbons. That, too, looked fabulous on her. On me—or 99.9 percent of the world's population—it would have looked like a terrible blunder from the craft factory. No doubt she'd sell at least two or three today to people who admired it on her.

"Don't wait too long," she warned. "That little waitress at Tea on Tap has been eyeing him lately."

"What's the tea lady doing in the coffee shop? Scoping out the competitor?"

Lilly gave me one of those pitying looks she saves for when she thinks I'm being particularly obtuse. Usually I get them when we're talking fashion.

"What else is happening on Pond Street? I seem to be out of touch."

"It's all those animals you surround yourself with. It doesn't give you enough time for people." She studied me with a surgical glare. "You need a date that doesn't have four legs and a tail."

"Shhh. Don't say that too loud. Bentley might hear. You know how sensitive he is."

I was only half kidding. I rescued Bentley from a shelter. He'd been abused in his former home and, in my *professional* opinion—such as it is—Bentley has serious self-esteem and confidence issues. These may also stem from the fact that he's not the most intimidating presence on the block. Or in the pet store. Or anywhere. He may resemble a pit bull somewhat, but his heart is pure powder puff. I'm sure I saved Bentley from extinction. Nobody else would have been crazy enough to adopt a dog like him. He knows that and has committed the rest of his life to loving me—what a great swap.

Happily, Lilly ignored me and began to fill me in on the latest from the rumor mill on Pond Street.

"Belles & Beaux is adding another masseuse."

Belles & Beaux is a day spa located in a huge restored Victorian up the street. It started out as a hair salon with two stations and a lot of out-of-date magazines, but has rapidly become a very chic and stylish spot. Then again, everything along Pond Street is becoming that way. The Bookworm now has author signings and poetry readings, the Drug Store's old soda fountain is *the* place for kids to hang out and, much to Joe's dismay, you can buy a latte at Barney's gas station right along with your unleaded premium.

Someday I'm hoping that Barney will realize that his sign, *Barney's Gas,* isn't quite specific enough. I've had more than one person come into my shop laughing and ask what kind of gas Barney has, anyway. I usually leave that question alone. It's an *explosive* issue.

"The store beyond Belles & Beaux has been sold to someone who's planning to open a toy shop."

"Cool." A toy store—my kind of people.

"And guess who said hello to me when I was at the Corner Market today?"

"Sorry, I can't. I left my mind-reading kit at home today."

"Connor Trevain. *Commander* Connor Trevain." She said it in the tone of an awestruck groupie.

"Back for a visit, huh?" *Commander* Connor owns the fleet of cruise boats that sail Lake Zachary, although he's never spent much time in Shoreside. He actually was a commander in the navy, a graduate of the Naval Academy and served as a ship's captain. It was well known that he "came from money," as Auntie Lou would say. They are fabulous boats. The largest, *The Zachary Zephyr,* is regularly rented for weddings, anniversaries and class reunions. The food and service are amazing and the surroundings romantic. It's a *très chic* place to be married. The smaller boats take tourists sightseeing around Lake Zachary, sometimes stopping at Ziga's, a supper club the Trevain family owns on the far side of the lake.

"No. That's the best part!"

"I thought you said you saw him."

"Not that. The best part is that he's not here for a visit. He's here to stay!"

That made about as much sense as wearing Bermuda shorts to shovel snow. Last I'd heard he was suffering away his time with some boating venture in Hawaii. "Why?"

"He's decided to be 'hands on' with the business. Isn't that exciting? He plans to captain *The Zachary Zephyr.*"

"Well, shiver me timbers, think of that." I put my hands on my hips and stared at my friend. "So what?"

"So, he is *rich* and *handsome* and *single,* that's what!"

The sun came out and the fog in my brain cleared. "And you have eyes on him?"

"Both eyes. He's going to make the scenery around the lake more spectacular than ever."

"Are you interested in dating him?" I asked, never quite sure what direction Lilly is going with her rambling conversations. She's a smart girl but fixated on clothes and, occasionally, men.

"Are you kidding? Of course, but he won't look at the likes of us."

"'Us'? When did I get involved in this?"

She grabbed my hands. "Wouldn't it be wonderful if he asked one of *us* out?"

Her eyes got wide as two saucers. "I have to check to see what's on order for the store. I'll need new clothes. Who knows when I might run into him!" She eyed me up and down like a disapproving school marm. "It wouldn't hurt you to get something new, either." With a swirl of red, she shot back into her shop where, I knew, she'd spend the rest of the day poring over fashion magazines and doodling with her own clothing designs. I love Lilly. She's funny, beautiful and my polar opposite. For every fashionista outfit she has, I have a pair of denim jeans and a sweatshirt. Of course, she doesn't haul fifty pound bags of dog food, change litter boxes or deal with un-trained puppies in her business, either.

"And…"

I spun around to see Lilly poking her head out the door again.

"The new cop is on duty. We can all sleep well tonight." Then she disappeared again around the door jamb and didn't return.

Whew. Feeling as though I'd just been through a wind-storm of trivia, I shook myself off and went back to tending to the only business I should be minding, anyway.

*Love Inspired*

# BLISSFULLY YOURS

BY

# DIANN WALKER

*A Special
Steeple Hill Café novel
in Love Inspired*

Who would refuse a friend?
Not Gwen Sandler, who
took time off from teaching
to help her friend's brother,
Mitch Windsor, open a ski
resort. Gwen was looking
to add some excitement to
her life, but did that mean
risking her heart, too?

*Available June 2006
wherever you buy books.*

Steeple
Hill
Café

# An Unexpected Blessing

BY

# Merrillee Whren

Dori Morales had been caring for her nephew since the tragic deaths of his parents. To protect little JT from a fierce custody battle, she agreed to marry his long-lost uncle, Chase Garrett. But would love come after marriage and the baby carriage?

*Available June 2006 wherever you buy books.*

**www.SteepleHill.com**

Steeple Hill®

LIAUB

# 2 Love Inspired novels and a mystery gift... Absolutely FREE!

Visit

## www.LoveInspiredBooks.com

for your two FREE books, sent directly to you!

**BONUS:** Choose between regular print or our NEW larger print format!

There's no catch! You're under no obligation to buy anything. We charge nothing—ZERO—for your first shipment. And you don't have to make any minimum number of purchases.

You'll like the convenience of home delivery at our special discount prices, and you'll love your free subscription to Steeple Hill News, our members-only newsletter.

We hope that after receiving your free books, you'll want to remain a subscriber. But the choice is yours— to continue or cancel, anytime at all! So why not take us up on our invitation, with no risk of any kind!

*Love Inspired*®